RED SHOE DIARIES

Red Shoe Diaries

Zalman's King's

RED SHOE DIARIES

Another Woman's Lipstick

Novelization by Elise D'Haene & Stacey Donovan

BASED ON THE TELEPLAYS

- ◆ "Red Shoe Diaries"
  written by Patricia Louisianna Knop & Zalman King

- ◆ "Just Like That"
  written by Chloe King

- ◆ "Another Woman's Lipstick"
  written by Ed Silverstein

- ◆ "Talk to Me, Baby"
  written by Zalman King

AND THE ORIGINAL STORY

- ◆ "Sex in the Hamptons: The Writers' Confessions"
  written by Elise D'Haene & Stacey Donovan

BERKLEY BOOKS, NEW YORK

THE BERKLEY PUBLISHING GROUP
Published by the Penguin Group
Penguin Group (USA) Inc.
375 Hudson Street, New York, New York 10014, USA
Penguin Group (Canada), 90 Eglinton Avenue, Suite 700, Toronto, Ontario M4P 2Y3, Canada
(a division of Pearson Penguin Canada Inc.)
Penguin Books Ltd., 80 Strand, London WC2R 0RL, England
Penguin Group (Ireland), 25 St. Stephen's Green, Dublin 2, Ireland (a division of Penguin Books Ltd.)
Penguin Group (Australia), 250 Camberwell Road, Camberwell, Victoria 3124, Australia
(a division of Pearson Australia Group Pty. Ltd.)
Penguin Books India Pvt. Ltd., 11 Community Centre, Panchsheel Park, New Delhi—110 017, India
Penguin Books (NZ), Cnr. Airborne and Rosedale Roads, Albany, Auckland 1310, New Zealand
(a division of Pearson New Zealand Ltd.)
Penguin Books (South Africa) (Pty.) Ltd., 24 Sturdee Avenue, Rosebank, Johannesburg 2196,
South Africa

Penguin Books Ltd., Registered Offices: 80 Strand, London WC2R 0RL, England

This book is an original publication of The Berkley Publishing Group.

PRINTING HISTORY
Berkley trade paperback edition / January 2006

Library of Congress Cataloging-in-Publication Data

D'Haene, Elise, 1959–
    Zalman King's red shoe diaries. Another woman's lipstick / novelization by Elise D'Haene & Stacey Donovan.—Berkley trade pbk ed.
        p.   cm.
    "Based on the teleplays "Red Shoe Diaries" written by Patricia Lousianna Knop & Zalman King ; "Just Like That" written by Chloe King ; "Another Woman's Lipstick" written by Ed Silverstein ; "Talk to Me, Baby" written by Zalman King ; and the original story "Sex in the Hamptons: The Writers' Confessions" written by Elise D'Haene & Stacey Donovan."
    ISBN 0-425-20756-0 (pbk.)
    1. Erotic stories, American. I. Title: Another woman's lipstick. II. Donovan, Stacey. III. King, Zalman. IV. Red shoe diaries (Television program). V. Title.

PS3554.H25Z24 2006
813'.54—dc22   2005027487

PRINTED IN THE UNITED STATES OF AMERICA

10   9   8   7   6   5   4   3   2   1

Contents

◆

RED SHOE DIARIES

WOMEN

Do you keep a diary?
Have you been betrayed?
Have you betrayed another?
Man, 35, wounded and alone,
recovering from loss
of a once in a lifetime love
looking for reasons why.

Send diaries to Red Shoes, P.O. Box 315,
Los Angeles, CA 90203

Just Like That

◆

JAKE

How do I look, Stella? Too casual? Too stiff? You're right—lose the tie. I'm going out, not to a meeting. You know, Stella, there's a Lassie marathon on TV Land. I could stay home, order a pizza, share a six-pack with you. Woof. What, you want alone time? Fine. I guess you're entitled to a little separation, some solitude, like we all are. . . .

I'm at the bar at Michael's, a Venice Beach neighborhood bistro and a hangout for young, professional singles—at least that's what Paul said on the job site yesterday. I'm drinking a martini—Bombay Sapphire, three olives. The first drink always loosens the tension I drag around with me like an appendage. The bartender is my age—a handsome guy, I guess, probably an actor. Groups of hip and sexy women exchange glances with groups of less hip, less sexy men. I'm pretty much the only solo player at the bar. How does anyone meet anyone in a place like this without sounding like a jerk? "Hi, I'm Jake. You look amazing." "I couldn't help but notice that shade of lipstick you're wearing." "I'm Jake. Can I buy you a drink?" Sure, asshole.

I met Alex in a used-record store in Santa Monica. We were both flipping through albums. We reached for the same one at the same moment—the first release of the first the Mamas and the Papas album. On the cover they're all in a bathtub next to a toilet. In the second release of the album, the toilet was removed. It was quite a find. I begged her to let me have it, confessing that I had a wild crush on Mama Cass, even if she was dead. She laughed, said she too had a boner for Cass. That was it—as easy as that. We split the cost of the album, went back to her studio apartment with wine and beef burritos, and sang along to "Monday, Monday," "California Dreamin'," and "I Call Your Name."

But you're not here, Alex. You're not here. What am I doing here? The second martini can go either of two ways: One, release me from all inhibitions; two, ignite anger. Tonight it's number two. I hit the air and head down the sidewalk toward the water. Abbot Kinney is a long boulevard in the heart of Venice populated by designers, boutiques, restaurants, and art galleries. I pass them by without registering a thing, nor do I notice the people sharing the sidewalk with me. I just want to feel at home in my goddamned bones for one goddamned minute.

I hit the boardwalk and I'm punched by the noise, the mob of people selling and buying T-shirts, sunglasses, drinking too much in outdoor cafés, Rollerblading, jogging. Boom boxes blast rap and young ethnic dancers show off their moves. A juggler tosses chainsaws up into the air and for a split second I'm tempted to get in his way, cause an accident in which my head is tragically severed from my body.

I begin to run, my feet on a sudden mission. The destination is the darkening Pacific Ocean. The sunset casts the water in deep maroon, an inky throbbing mass. I take off my shoes and socks, step into the liquid and feel the wet sand creep between my toes. I pull in the salty air, filling my gut. When was the last time I breathed so deeply?

I walk for a while, no thoughts, just sensations. The wind. The sand beneath my weight. The whoosh of water greeting the shore, then retreating.

I finally make my way back, taking a small side street that leads to Ocean Boulevard. Brightly painted California bungalows line the street.

A FOR SALE BY OWNER sign catches my attention, seems to call to me. The lights are on inside the sky-blue home trimmed in yellow. Orange rocking chairs are perched on the front porch. I skip up the steps, my feet taking over, as if they don't belong to me but belong on these steps leading to this unknown house.

An older woman opens the door. She appears to be in her early seventies; her face is tan and tender.

"I'd like to buy your house." The words just spill out of me. "I'm sorry to disturb you."

"Come in, young man," she says, without a hint of irritation at my disruption.

I've been living in a tomb, a mausoleum dedicated to Alex's memories. At night, downtown Los Angeles is quiet and empty and we used to pretend the whole city belonged only to us. I don't want to be in that loft anymore. I want to be here. I call your name, Alex, but you're not there anymore.

◆ ◆ ◆

Dear Red Shoes,

Try to envision a train on a track. One direction. No diversions. No time for delay. I was just like that: I worked during the day, and at night, I went to law school. My life was completely planned out. Very organized, very predictable. And then the unexpected happened, forcing me off the track and into a head-on collision . . . with myself.

You will be my judge, Red Shoes, and I will not only prosecute myself, I will also serve as my own defense attorney. Your ad states: *Have you been betrayed? Have you betrayed another?* I charge myself with betrayal, deception, dishonesty, licentiousness (pursuing desires aggressively and selfishly, unchecked by morality, especially in sexual matters), and finally, of negligence.

COURT OF THE RED SHOE DIARIES

TRUDIE BROOKS, Plaintiff,
v.   **Case No. 06.920**
TRUDIE BROOKS, Defendant

Trudie Brooks (almost Esq.)
Attorney for Plaintiff and Defendant.

PROSECUTING ATTORNEY: May it please the court, I would like to call my first witness, Trudie Brooks.

Ms. Brooks, do you swear to tell the truth, the whole truth, and nothing but the truth, so help you God?

TRUDIE: I'll try.

PA: I hope you realize, young lady, that the charges brought against you are serious and that this court will prove, beyond a reasonable doubt, that your actions, decisions, and willful intent have caused irreparable harm to the very fabric of our society. Ms. Brooks, may I call you Trudie?

TRUDIE: Please do.

PA: You are studying for the bar exam?

TRUDIE: That's correct.

PA: And you work a full-time job at the legal firm of Denom, Dillon, and Tate?

TRUDIE: Yes.

PA: What is your position at the firm?

TRUDIE: Receptionist.

PA: Isn't it true that at the firm, you assumed several lewd positions as well?

DEFENSE ATTORNEY: Objection, Your Honor. Badgering.
(Well, Red Shoes, do you have a ruling? I'd say, "sustained." The prosecutor was being nasty, wouldn't you agree?)

PA: While working at Denom, Dillon, and Tate, did you have an encounter with Kyle Cusomono?

TRUDIE: Several. He's a messenger. He would deliver . . . packages and messages daily.

PA: Would you please describe Kyle?

TRUDIE: He's adorable—a boyish Matt LeBlanc, with a smile as wide as the ocean. And a body dreamed up by a god— muscled, tan, not too big, just perfect.

PA: And Mr. Phillipe?

TRUDIE: Not Mr. Phillipe—just Phillipe.

PA: And you are acquainted with Phillipe?

TRUDIE: Of course. He's a client of the firm.

PA: So you know him?

TRUDIE: Intimately.

PA: Can you describe Phillipe for the court?

TRUDIE: Self-assured. Sophisticated. Mysterious. Powerful.

PA: And he's considerably older—

DA: Objection. Irrelevant.

TRUDIE: [blurting] He's forty-five. I'm twenty-eight. Who cares?

PA: And Kyle, how old is he?

TRUDIE: Twenty-one.

PA: Your Honor, I'd like to refer to deposition twelve by Kyle Cusomono, regarding his account of his relationship with Ms. Brooks.

DA: No objections.

PA: Mr. Cusomono—Kyle—asked you out for lunch on one June the third. Is that correct?

TRUDIE: Yes.

PA: And you turned him down?

TRUDIE: Yes.

PA: And then he asked you out for dinner?

TRUDIE: Yes.

PA: And you turned him down?

TRUDIE: Work. Classes. Bar exam. You do the math.

PA: Your Honor, the witness is being argumentative.

DA: Objection. The witness is answering truthfully. She had a lot on her fucking plate.

TRUDIE: You can say that again.

(Red Shoes: You'll have to allow for a bit of legal leeway here. I really want to make it clear that I was under tremendous pressure, the kind you don't even know you're under until something happens, just like that, and you're tumbling and turning and craving chaos and mayhem and even madness. . . . Know what I mean? The end of your rope, as they say.)

PA: Trudie, were you attracted to Kyle?

TRUDIE: Of course. He's irresistible.

PA: So why did you turn him down?

DA: Objection. Already established. Full plate.

PA: Isn't it true that Kyle whispered something into your ear that day and that you followed him into the elevator *after* you had turned him down for lunch?

TRUDIE: Yes.

PA: What did he whisper?

TRUDIE: [whispers] "Every time I jerk off, I'm thinking of you . . . and only you."

PA: Will you repeat that?

TRUDIE: [louder] "Every time I jerk off, I'm thinking of you . . . and only you."

PA: And how did you respond?

TRUDIE: My nipples ached. Almost as if I could hear them moan.

PA: So you entered the elevator, and Kyle said—I'm referring to page two, paragraph ten in the deposition—"Is it still today or is it tomorrow? It must be tomorrow. It can't be today because today you were too busy to have lunch." Is that correct?

TRUDIE: Yes.

PA: And what did you say?

TRUDIE: "Well, I guess I was hungrier than I thought."

PA: And then what happened?

TRUDIE: The elevator started going down.

PA: What floor is Denom, Dillon, and Tate on?

TRUDIE: Seventy-five.

PA: Was anyone else in the elevator with you?

TRUDIE: No. Just Kyle, his bike, and me.

PA: Can you describe what happened next?

TRUDIE: I looked into his eyes. Did I describe his eyes? Azure blue, like the clear desert sky. He smiled. It was slow, deliberate, inviting, and even a little uncertain, as if his lips were asking, *What does she want?* Waiting for me to indicate my intent. . . .

PA: And did you indicate your intent?

TRUDIE: Yes. I went insane. I lunged at him. My lips collided with his, our tongues body slammed. He tasted like chili peppers. I thought I might swallow him whole. I was that ferocious. So unlike me, so out of character. My nipples were crushed against his brilliant, fucking mountainous chest, and now instead of moaning, my breasts were screaming.

PA: Excuse me, but nipples and breasts do not make sounds.

DA: Objection, Your Honor, the prosecutor is not an expert on the audible noises made by body parts. Fingers crack. Knees creak. Nipples moan.

TRUDIE: You have to understand, it had been a long, long time since I had had sex. I had silenced my body. My desire was mute. I *heard* the sounds. Maybe it was only in my imagination, but my imagination is a part of my reality and therefore, I did hear the sounds. Not only did my breasts scream, but from my vagina—my pussy, cunt, slash, slit, center of the universe—came a roar so loud, so immense, I felt as if the earth would tip on its axis and pieces of the sky might break off and crash into the ocean. That was the sound, Your Honor. If you can imagine that sound, then maybe you will begin to realize who I was at that very moment in time.

JAKE

Wow, Stella, this is one gripping letter. I feel the weight of the responsibility she's given to me. Judge her. Find her innocent. Find her guilty. She picked the right guy. I'm the supreme judge of my entire life—I still blame myself for Alex's death. It was emotional negligence, a failure on my part to exercise an ultimate sensitivity toward her that caused her to suffer the most severe of damages. Trudie is battling it out in a pretend courtroom, and yet the stakes feel almost dire for her. I will do my best to remain impartial and listen to the evidence. Maybe I'll even begin to hear the sounds in my own body that have been dead since Alex.

. . .

PA: Your words are very dramatic, Ms. Brooks, but let's stick to the facts. What happened after you kissed?

TRUDIE: I'm not finished with the kiss. Have you ever had a stranger's tongue explode in your mouth? That instant, that wet nanosecond, is like a birth, a seed cracking open. We ceased being strangers then, no words needed, just the language of desire that needs no translator.

PA: Can we please return to the elevator? What happened after you kissed?

TRUDIE: I saw the numbers on the elevator floors zipping past: sixty, fifty-nine, fifty-eight, and somehow those numbers— each floor we passed—marked a beginning, or an entry, into my existence as a living, breathing woman who had neglected her desires, her passions, her needs. I felt—

PA: *Please*, just answer the question. *What happened after you kissed?*

TRUDIE: Well, to be perfectly honest with you we didn't stop kissing, so I don't know how to answer your question.

PA: I'll rephrase. In the elevator, what else did you do with Kyle besides kissing?

DA: Objection. The details of her encounter are irr—

TRUDIE: No, I want to answer.

PA: [snickers] Your client has overruled your objection. Go on, Ms. Brooks.

TRUDIE: He threw me up against the wall of the elevator.

PA: Against your will?

TRUDIE: No. No. It's exactly what I wanted. He took me, by force. He reached under my dress, ripped off my panties, grabbed my ass, lifted me, my legs wrapped around his thighs. God, they were so tight, must be from riding his bike, so deliriously hard, muscles rippling against my skin, transferring a kind of stallion power that overwhelmed me. Maybe a stallion is cliché, but fuck it, Your Honor, he was wild. I'd eat grass in a prairie alongside him any day, lap from a stream, and let the wind sing in our ears as we charged across a vast field of wheat.

PA: Ms. Brooks. Trudie. Facts, please!

TRUDIE: These are my facts!

PA: Your Honor, the witness is hostile.

DA: You are badgering the witness, Counselor. Allow her to answer the question in her own way.

JAKE: *LET HER SPEAK! I understand why Trudie needs to say everything, anything, all of it—to be heard, understood, to have her words count, uncensored. She had crossed a line. She was plummeting, falling and tumbling, into the unknown, the unexpressed, the unplanned. Out of character, as she put it. Goddamn it, clinging to character is exactly what ruined my life, ruined my love for Alex. Destroyed us. So as the judge in this case, I say: Let her speak!*

PA: Very well. Go on and on, Ms. Brooks, about your yelping vagina.

DA: Objection. It was screaming, not yelping.

PA: I recant. Proceed.

TRUDIE: Thank you. I unclasped his belt as he ripped open the condom package with his teeth. I snapped open his Levi's, plunged my hand inside. He wasn't wearing any briefs. His cock was hot to the touch, swelling against my palm. It was like holding something alive, like a rock simmering under the sun, and . . .

PA: A rock is not alive.

TRUDIE: All matter is energy, Counselor. Or did you skip the class on quantum physics? Forty-one, forty, thirty-nine . . . My god, we were free-falling through space, unchained from gravity. I yanked his Levi's down and his cock saluted the air. He slid the lubricated condom onto it and then thrust his missile into the mouth of my cunt. Open and dripping. Wide and consuming. Drenched and ravenous. He continued to grip my ass and hammered me over and over. God, it hurt.

PA: He hurt you?

TRUDIE: Oh, yeah, he hurt me. His balls smacked my ass. His fingernails dug into my skin. And he drilled my cunt as if I were concrete. Oh, yeah, he hurt me. Twenty-one, twenty, nineteen . . . I was a woman in a metal box with a man, and inside that space, careening toward the earth, I shed every dead molecule that I'd been dragging around for years. Dead. Dead. Dead. Do you understand? I needed the pain. I had to be thrashed. Pounded. Pummeled.

PA: Are you a masochist, Ms. Brooks?

TRUDIE: Pleasure in pain? Why define it? If someone's heart stops beating and you pound on his chest to revive him, or you zap him with violent volts of electricity, would you say that is sadism? No, it's restoring life. Masochism works the same way. My clit understood that.

PA: So now your clit has a brain?

TRUDIE: In a way, yes. A consciousness. Where do the signals of desire come from? Our synapses. And those signals are carried through the body. So, yes, my clit understood.

I put my fingers into Kyle's mouth, slathering them with his spicy spit, then began slapping that ignored nub, a seed forgotten.

PA: Excuse me, for clarification: You were slapping your clit?

TRUDIE: My clit. It was hard and pulsing, wet from the slick smacking of our fucking. From both of us, guttural, jarring groans reverberated off the walls. His cock was titanic inside of me, like I was the sky and he was the Goodyear Blimp. Ten, nine, eight . . .

PA: Don't you think you are overstating the size of his member?

TRUDIE: His member was inside my hole, not yours.

PA: Go on.

TRUDIE: I remember I licked his face—his sweat was tangy and sugary at the same time. My tongue drank him in, his nectar sliding down my throat, into my belly, and I howled, knowing this couldn't last forever. He didn't know why I was howling, but he joined me. Suddenly, I swung my arm and punched the red emergency button; the elevator jerked to a stop and the alarm bell rang.

PA: At what floor?

TRUDIE: Six, I think. I really don't remember. I clenched the walls of my cunt as hard as I could, a vice grip around his fucking massive power and I could feel it—another wet nanosecond right before detonation. I was working my clit hard, and we both came in sync, grunting in rhythm. His hot seed filled the condom and my juices tumbled like a waterfall around him. Wow.

PA: That was it?

TRUDIE: That was it. He lifted me off his cock and without a word we got dressed. Kyle pulled the emergency stop, and the elevator descended to the lobby.

I entered that box as one woman. And when I reached the ground, I was a completely different woman. Unrecognizable to myself. What a glorious feeling.

PA: Did you feel even remotely guilty?

TRUDIE: No.

PA: Not one moment of regret?

TRUDIE: No.

PA: What is your attitude toward anonymous sex?

DA: Objection. My client is not a sociologist.

JAKE: *Overruled. She can share her opinion about an act she has just participated in.*

TRUDIE: I'd never had anonymous sex before, although, Kyle wasn't a complete stranger. I didn't know his name, but he'd been in the office at least a dozen times before. I mean, think about the word "anonymous." One definition is to obscure someone's identity. Many lovers obscure their identities from each other. Another definition is to allow someone to go unnoticed. Often, the person you're having sex with goes unnoticed, barely registers with you—he becomes just a body without a soul. A body used for pleasure without regard. So maybe people, without even realizing it, are having anonymous sex all the time.

PA: You're being evasive, Ms. Brooks. Before your encounter with Kyle, what were your attitudes toward sex between two strangers?

TRUDIE: Before Kyle, you could say that when I masturbated I was having sex with a stranger.

PA: You're not answering my question.

DA: Objection. She's answered. It may not be the answer Counsel wants to hear, but it is an honest response.

JAKE: *Sustained. I like her answers.*

PA: All right, all right, let's move on. On page five, paragraph six of Mr. Cusomono's deposition, he reports that he got out of the elevator with his bike and left the building. What did you do next?

TRUDIE: I stayed on the elevator and a bunch of suits got in with me. Just as the doors were about to close, I heard a familiar voice calling out: "Hold the doors, please."

PA: And who was it?

TRUDIE: Phillipe.

PA: Isn't it true, Ms. Brooks, that after you fucked one man, you immediately accepted an invitation to lunch from another? Namely, this Phillipe person?

TRUDIE: Yes.

PA: Care to elaborate?

TRUDIE: I was really hungry, as you can imagine.

PA: And you also accepted his invitation for dinner that very night?

TRUDIE: Yes.

PA: No class? No studying for the bar exam?

TRUDIE: Out of character, I know. But, remember, I had changed, just like that.

PA: Phillipe is an attorney and a client at the firm where you are employed?

TRUDIE: Yes.

PA: Would you admit that you seduced him in order to climb the corporate ladder?

DA: OBJECTION! Badgering the witness.

JAKE: *Sustained.*

TRUDIE: I don't need to fuck a man to succeed! Everything I've accomplished I've done on my own, without help—financial or otherwise.

PA: Did you have sexual intercourse with Phillipe that first night?

TRUDIE: Well, I, uh—

PA: Are you familiar with the term *malum in se*?

TRUDIE: Of course. It's Latin, referring to an act that is wrong in itself, in its very nature illegal because it violates the natural, moral, or public principles of a civilized society.

DA: Your Honor, where is this going?

JAKE: *I'm interested in finding out. Continue.*

PA: Having sex with two men you barely know in one day—don't you consider that immoral behavior for a civilized woman?

TRUDIE: I . . . uh, well, it's . . .

PA: Don't you think most civilized people would consider your behavior sluttish?

DA: Objection!

JAKE: *Sustained. That was a low blow. Strike it from the record.*

TRUDIE: I have the power to do whatever I want with my body.

PA: So does a whore.

JAKE: *Easy, Counselor, or I'll find you in contempt.*

PA: Did your cunt scream with Phillipe, too?

TRUDIE: No . . . It sang. Sultry, like Nina Simone. Sex with Phillipe was slow and warm like brandy. Like candle wax dripping onto a marble floor. Like the glowing embers of a fire, long after the flames are gone, pulsing with heat. His tongue was languid and smooth and it strolled across my skin, absorbing all of me. He could caress my hand and the walls of my pussy would ache. His mouth grazing my nipple could make me come. The flutter of his eyelashes when he gazed at me made my slit a long, lazy river. He would have me crawl across the floor to him, licking my lips, swaying my hips, rocking my breasts back and forth, and then tell me to stop. Freeze. Not to move.

PA: Excuse me for interrupting your reverie, but I'd like to return to some semblance of order in the events related to the charges against you.

TRUDIE: Okay.

PA: When did you begin lying?

DA: Objection.

JAKE: *Overruled. The defendant is accused of deception.*

TRUDIE: I began lying right away, to both Kyle and Phillipe. One heart, two beats. Double the dilemma. Two times the confusion. Kyle and Phillipe. Phillipe and Kyle. I was breaking all the rules.

PA: Would you characterize your problem as nymphomania?

TRUDIE: NO!

PA: Sex! Sex! Sex! Just couldn't get—

DA: OBJECTION.

PA: Couldn't get enough! Had to have it! Why stop at two men?

DA: Objection, your Honor, please. Badgering.

JAKE: *Sustained. I'm fining you five hundred dollars for your antics, Counselor.*

PA: I accept your condemnation, but I'm not on trial here. She is.

TRUDIE: Then give me a chance to tell my story. I was entranced by Phillipe and crazy for Kyle. I mean, have you ever crawled across the floor naked toward someone—a man, a woman— who worships you? And Phillipe would tell me to stop, and I would stop. Feeling a deepening, simmering heat flush my skin, from the tips of my toes to the top of my head. "Kiss your wrist," he would whisper. My lips felt the rush of blood in my veins, and with my tongue I would trace a trail up my arm, gently tasting myself, falling in love with myself.

PA: And what was Phillipe doing?

TRUDIE: Watching me. Guiding me. "Hold your breasts," he commanded. They were pillow soft, two handfuls, heavy and buoyant at the same time. "Squeeze them. Look at them." My own hands were making love to my body as if I were a virgin.

"Touch your nipples." I held each between my thumb and index finger. "Softly," he demanded.

"Close your eyes. See me, seeing you." I did. I closed my eyes. A hum of desire filled the air between us. A palpable energy growing in the space between us, ten feet, maybe fifteen, but I was more connected to him in those moments than I'd ever felt with anyone before.

"Tell me what you see," he said. Behind the veil of my eyelids, as my fingers sighed against my nipples, I saw heart-wrenching vulnerability and undeniable power. No wonder men want to be inside a woman. No wonder they often have to denigrate us as they worship us. No wonder God banished Adam and Eve because He gave that first woman more power than even He could take. Out of our cunts comes creation. From our breasts comes nourishment, sustenance. We have *everything*.

I imagined, with my eyes closed, sliding my own tongue up inside of me, traveling into that silken wet womb, circling my own clit with my own slick fingers. Tongue inching deeper. A finger playing my swollen, swelling, deep pink pearl, and all the while my voice moans and those moans fill my body like a song, an aria, a shattering opera of love. . . .

PA: Ms. Brooks? Ms. Brooks?

TRUDIE: Yes.

PA: Open your eyes, please.

TRUDIE: Oh. Sorry, I lost myself. Where was I?

PA: On the floor. Touching your breasts.

TRUDIE: My eyes were still closed, and from behind me, I heard Phillipe sigh. Light as a feather, his finger caressed my clit, barely perceptible, just a hint of contact that made my thighs tremble and my breasts quiver beneath my hands. "On your knees, beauty."

I rose to my knees, my face resting on a blanket on the floor. His hands parted my ass cheeks and all at once, my whole body was suffused with indescribable joy as his tongue glided up the slope from my unexplored hole to my dripping well. He returned to my asshole, circling it slowly, then lapping, increasing the pressure with his tongue. His rough cheeks added to the delicious friction. My whole body shuddered. A long, eternal *"ahhhhhh"* escaped from my mouth.

I was under a spell—an erotic hallucination of absolute ecstasy. I began to swing my head back and forth like a bell being struck for the very first time, the sound echoing through the whole universe.

One. Two. Three. Now, his fingers were inside my cunt, matching the motions of his stabbing tongue as he pressed deeper inside of me. With his other hand, he thrummed expertly against my burgeoning clit.

"Release it all to me, beauty," he whispered. I was floating in space, careening down the rapids of a warm river, swooping through the sky on a current of wind. Every infinitesimal speck of my being was writhing and wild, and I cried out when I came, tears bursting from my eyes. Phillipe held me and rocked me, whispering how beautiful I was. "Such immeasurable power, so delicate, so full of grace." That was my first experience with him.

PA: Did he penetrate you with his member?

TRUDIE: Not that night.

PA: Did you perform fellatio on him?

TRUDIE: No, not that night.

PA: While you were with Phillipe *that night*, did you think about Kyle and your experience with him *that day*?

TRUDIE: No. That was a different planet, like another dimension in time and space.

PA: Did you have occasion to see Mr. Cusomono again?

TRUDIE: Yes, the next day.

PA: He made a delivery?

TRUDIE: Yes.

PA: Anything more than that?

TRUDIE: He asked me to lunch.

PA: And you agreed?

TRUDIE: Yes.

PA: Did lunch include food?

DA: Objection! Lunch implies food.

JAKE: *Overruled. The obvious.*

TRUDIE: Not this lunch. We didn't eat . . . food.

PA: Please describe the circumstances of your second meeting with Mr. Cusomono.

TRUDIE: Isn't it in his deposition?

PA: His accounting is brief. It says, on page eight, paragraph six, "It was hot."

TRUDIE: I would agree with his description.

PA: Elaborate, Ms. Brooks.

TRUDIE: It was a lovely day, really, and it's hard to be cooped up in an office when the sun is so inviting. So we went up to the roof. I'm friendly with the maintenance supervisor and—

PA: Friendly sexual or friendly friendly?

TRUDIE: Door number two. So he gave us access to the roof.

PA: And what happened on the roof?

TRUDIE: Kyle is not just a delivery man, he's an actor. He was auditioning for a role as a sadistic cop named Roy, who is blackmailing a married woman whom he is sexually obsessed with, so he brought along some props for us to play with.

PA: Props?

TRUDIE: A fake gun. Handcuffs. A billy club. He read his lines and I improvised my part as the woman. I helped him rehearse.

PA: And did helping him rehearse also include sexual activity?

TRUDIE: That's what the script called for.

PA: What kind of sexual activity?

TRUDIE: Pretty outrageous stuff. Violent. Nasty. Sick.

PA: And you condone violent, nasty, sick sex?

TRUDIE: We were acting. To tell you the truth, Kyle is so boyish that I didn't think he could pull off such a sinister character. But in the end, he was quite impressive.

PA: Describe, in detail, the scene that you participated in.

TRUDIE: On the way up to the roof, after he asked if I would help him rehearse, he said, "You have to trust me. Just go along." So, the moment we stepped out of the stairwell and onto the roof, he grabbed my arm, slapped a cuff onto my wrist, and dragged me to a utility pole, attaching me to it.

PA: He had you locked to the pole?

TRUDIE: Yes.

PA: Were you at all afraid?

TRUDIE: I was excited, maybe a little afraid, but that was because Kyle was completely in character.

PA: Go on.

TRUDIE: He was speaking calmly. It was chilling at first. He was stroking the club, and then began to use it to undress me. With one hand he unbuttoned my blouse, then pulled the fabric aside with the stick, exposing my breasts. I was wearing a black lace bra, and he glided the baton along my cleavage as he unzipped the back of my skirt.

PA: Do you recall his words?

TRUDIE: Oh yes, because later that night, on the phone, I helped him with his memorization. He continued to undress me as he spoke.

[Deepening her voice] "It's your fault, baby. You know that. The way you looked at me, standing real close at the grocery store, that day we first met. I could tell, in your eyes, you knew I could smell your pussy. You wanted me to smell it. You dropped that box of Juicy Juice on purpose, bending over, wanting me to fuck you, to smell your crotch, all steamy, like a muddy Louisiana pond in late August. Then you got afraid, like all you bitches do. . . ."

He was pressing that long black club against my panties, rubbing it up and down, and suddenly he shoved it under the elastic and ripped the panties off of me. Just like that.

He reared his arm back, his eyes flashing with rage, and I flinched, believing he was going to strike me. Instead, he knelt and softly caressed my face, holding the baton between my legs.

"It could be us, just the two of us, forever. I could tell, seeing you that time at the café, when you glanced up at me as you took a bite of a fry. I could see it, by the way you moved your mouth, how your lips parted wide when you laughed at what your kid said, that all you wanted was my meat shoved so deep down your throat you'd almost stop breathing. Tell me I'm right, Lana, tell me that's what you wanted."

This is where my character, Lana, says her line, except at the time I was improvising. So I said, "Please, let me go. I won't tell the police."

"I SAID tell me what you wanted!" he screamed.

Then Kyle broke character and told me that at this point in the script, he's already killed her husband and kidnapped her little boy, Joey. All she wants is to know where Joey is being held. That helped me with my motivation—I'd do anything to get my son back.

"Please, Roy, I got to have it, got to have you! You're right. I lied to you. I only want you. Fuck me, Roy. Fuck me hard. Show me how much you love me. Give it to me, baby. God, I want it so bad."

He put the baton in his mouth, drooled his spit across the tip, and slowly began pressing it into that hot pond between my legs.

"Oh, yeah," I said, "I can take it. Whatever you've got."

"Beg for it, cunt. Beg."

"Please, please, take off these cuffs so I can feel you get hard. I want you to put your fat rod into my mouth, lap those furry, luscious balls with my tongue."

"Just you and me, baby. Forever."

He started to undo the handcuffs when I said, "Just you, me, and Joey. We'll be a family."

"No fucking kid!" he snapped. He relocked the cuffs and pulled out his gun, shoving it between my lips as he pushed the baton deeper inside of me.

I was surprised how easily the walls of my cunt accepted it, wanted it, squeezed it hard, inviting him to go even farther. I saw this long, black object sticking out between my legs and it was as if I had my own massive twelve-inch dick. I had never even strapped on a dildo before, so you can understand, visually, how stunning it was.

"Fuck it," he commanded.

He cocked the gun and twisted it inside my mouth while

he stroked the black stick as if he was jerking off. I raised my ass off the roof, bouncing my hips. I had to have more. Wanted it deep and hard and unforgiving.

At this point, Kyle was fully clothed, but he couldn't take it anymore. He shoved down his jeans and there it was, his prick pointed at me like an impatient weapon.

"I'm gonna fuck you, bitch, fuck you till you're dead, then fuck you some more."

He withdrew the gun from my mouth, tossed it aside.

I spat in his face, "You don't have what it takes, pussy!"

I was pretty impressed with that line. Kyle was, too, because he broke character and said, "Wow, cool."

I continued: "You wimp! Can't even take me without these cuffs. Fucking pissant nobody!"

He unlocked the cuffs, and I began to pummel his chest with my fists, screaming and raging, "I hate you! I'll kill you!"

I caught him a little off guard, I think. That gave me time to yank the baton out of my pussy and slam it into his gut, pretending to do it hard. He reared back, totally in character, grunted, doubled over, and I scrambled for the gun. I grabbed it, turned, but Kyle was already on top of me. We wrestled. A shot of adrenaline rushed through me, and I fought back hard as he tried to get me to release the gun. His dick was raw, erect, and thrashing against my thigh. I cried out as I scraped my elbow against the asphalt roof.

"Fuck!" I yelled.

Taking that as a command, he pinned down my arms, rammed his cock into my gushing gash and beat me with it, over and over, harder, faster. Our mouths seized each other's, teeth scraping lips, whipping tongues, our hot saliva mixing and dripping off our chins.

We came fast—wild, feral, rough. I guess what Kyle had said in his deposition was accurate: It. Was. Hot.

PA: [clearing his throat] Yes. Okay. Uh. Now, Ms. Brooks, can you describe for the court what happened next?

TRUDIE: We got dressed. Gathered our belongings. He kept my torn panties and I kept the nightstick. Sentimental reasons, I guess. I had to get back to work and so did Kyle. Oh, and he did the dearest thing. He had a small first-aid kit in his backpack for the occasional mishap when he falls off of his bike, swerving in and out of traffic. He cleaned my scraped elbow with ointment, kissed it, and put a bandage on. The whole time he was humming a lullaby, probably like his mom used to do when he was little. It was lovely, just lovely.

PA: For the record, Ms. Brooks, you now had three separate sexual encounters with two men within a twenty-four hour period. Is that correct?

TRUDIE: Amazing, isn't it? Almost eighteen months and nothing but a vibrator between my legs once a week, if that, and all at once, there I was, fucking my brains out. And I now know why they say that: fucking your brains out. It's accurate. My brain had been on overdrive for so long—law school, work, studying for the bar. Another part of my anatomy had to take over to give my poor, tired intellect a break.

PA: Which part of your anatomy are you referring to?

TRUDIE: Any part of me that did not require logical thinking was up for this quite unexpected erotic adventure.

PA: Weren't you putting your academic and professional future in possible jeopardy?

TRUDIE: Perhaps.

PA: In fact, you accuse yourself of being reckless and decadent, acting out behavior completely unchecked by morality.

TRUDIE: Yes, but my morality was changing.

PA: You mean nonexistent!

DA: Objection.

JAKE: *Sustained. I'd like to take a break and reconvene in one hour.*

JAKE

I had to take Stella on our beach walk and digest Trudie's story.

It felt as if the gavel had landed upon my own head. It was Alex, not me, who had pushed the boundaries of our sexual life, our love-making, taking it from the expected into the unexpected. At times, I resisted, judged her desire as crossing the line. Where did that line come from? Who decides what kinds of physical expression are unacceptable between two consenting adults?

We had gone to Lake Tahoe for a long weekend and we were hiking in the woods when we came upon two deer fucking. It was spring, and all of nature's creatures were in heat. Naturally, I thought it was a male and female, but Alex crouched down and saw more clearly.

"Look at that," she whispered, pointing. "Two females. Look at those gorgeous, huge, red, oozing gashes."

One female had mounted the other, bucked and writhed, then hopped off. They kissed, nuzzled and rubbed their mouths against each other's necks. For me, there was something oddly repellent in what we were witnessing, but Alex got turned on. What was my problem? Nature unleashed in such a blatant, untamed manner? Too exposed?

As the deer continued to make out, Alex slid her hand under her sweats. "I'm wet just from watching them," she whispered. "Let's fuck now. Right here. With them."

Something tightened in my chest, a judgment, an embarrass-ment—even some shame attached to Alex being aroused by the deer, her animalistic instinct unleashed. On purpose, I stepped on a felled branch, cracking it with my boot startling the deer. They bolted.

"Shit," Alex said.

"Sorry, babe," I replied.

We're all creatures. All guided by biological impulses to mate. In the absence of a mate, we masturbate. The two female deer enacted what nature dictated.

Guilt is like bile in our brains, annihilating what is most essential in our humanness. I could have plunged my cock into Alex's wet well and taken her savagely in the woods as the two females took each other. Instead, I created a ruse to stop the rhythm of life, censor it, and make it disappear, then waited until we returned to our cabin to fuck, protected by the walls of my inhibition.

Stella crouched and peed on the sand at the beach. She sniffed a shell, licked the carcass of a dead fish. My little pup, you don't feel shame, do you? I asked. She wagged, nuzzled her nose against my crotch. I scratched her ears in the way I've learned she loves. I picked up a stick and tossed it into the water. She rushed after it—exuberant, instinctive, and joyful.

Back to the courtroom.

JAKE: *I'll remind you, Ms. Brooks, that you are still under oath.*

TRUDIE: Thank you, Your Honor.

PA: Ms. Brooks, did you consider consulting a professional psy-chologist to deal with your impulsive behavior?

TRUDIE: Honestly, no. Full-on fucking seemed to be the treat-ment I needed at the time.

PA: Are you familiar with the principles of Alcoholics Anonymous?

TRUDIE: No, not really.

PA: Regarding your sexual behavior, we've established that sex was disrupting your work life, your career goals, your studies. Correct?

TRUDIE: Yes.

PA: You've indicated that you felt out of character, perhaps out of control?

TRUDIE: Yes.

PA: That sex was driving the car of your life, metaphorically speaking, and not you?

TRUDIE: Well, I suppose.

PA: Would it be fair to say that you were obsessed with sex?

TRUDIE: Yes, that's fair.

PA: Sex was your drug of choice: your alcohol, your cocaine.

DA: Objection, Your Honor. Counsel is not, as far as I know, an expert on addiction or twelve-step programs.

JAKE: *Sustained. Wrap it up.*

TRUDIE: Your Honor, may I say something?

JAKE: *You may.*

TRUDIE: Before Kyle and Phillipe, my obsession was studying law. You could almost say I was compulsive—I never attended on-campus parties, accepted dates, went on vacations. No, I studied. The library was my second home. My job paid the bills. I was not living. I had reduced my existence to one thing only. You can't tell me that's healthy. I'm in my sexual prime, and I had placed my desire in a coffin. I am now attempting to defend my desire, to put myself on trial in order to fully understand what this experience has meant to me.

JAKE: *Thank you, Ms. Brooks. Counsel, you may continue with the witness.*

PA: After work, on the day you had your rooftop liaison with Mr. Cusomono, where did you go?

TRUDIE: To Phillipe's house. He was cooking me dinner.

PA: Describe the evening.

TRUDIE: When I arrived, he had already drawn me a bath. I was sore from my wrestling with Kyle, and the bath felt so soothing, so unimaginably blissful. I never took baths. My father insisted we shower, and quickly, because he was always concerned with the water bill. As a result, I believed that baths were a luxury that I couldn't afford to indulge in.

After the bath, Phillipe wrapped me in a soft, terry-cloth towel and guided me into the living room where flames blazed in the fireplace. He had pillows arranged on the floor in front of it, and he indicated that I should lie down.

He joined me and held a glass of red wine to my lips, silently offering me a sip.

"Spread your legs, beauty," he said.

I pulled the towel back, revealing my naked body. Those damned eyelashes of his fluttered as he gazed at all of me. My clit seemed to rise to meet his eyes as they drifted to my breasts.

"They are like two cathedrals, side by side, sacred places with domes of pleasure on top," he murmured.

His fingertips filtered through my pubes as he offered me a second drink of wine.

He put down the glass and picked up a tiny pair of sterling silver shears.

"I'm going to trim you a bit. Do you mind?" he asked.

"No, not at all," I replied.

Once again, his fingers brushed against my pussy. Delicately, with his thumb and index finger, he grasped my wheat-colored pubes and snipped them gently. He paused, grazed a finger against one supple, pliant labia, then the other. He parted them, his eyes completely intent on memorizing my pussy. A little trimming was followed by more soft strokes with his warm fingers. I watched, mesmerized by the care and focus of his attention. I could feel my bud growing, although he had not touched me there. Slight spasms flickered through me, and deep in my canal, slick juices seeped and trickled, causing a sweet tickling sensation within.

"It's like witnessing a rare orchid, one of a kind, discovered in a jungle," he said, as he lightly petted the swelling lips of my pussy. "Not many women," he continued, "realize how fantastically beautiful this fountain of creation is."

He rose to his knees, unzipped his slacks, and released his prick. I hadn't seen it before—it was so unlike Kyle's thick rod. Phillipe's was longer, more slender, with a deep coral hue. Refined and sophisticated, like he was, and powerful and mysterious, too. Droplets of milk glimmered like tiny pearls at the tip.

"I want you in my mouth," I murmured.

My suggestion urged forth a little bounce from his penis. Phillipe smiled and his eyes sparked with desire.

He leaned back against a chair. On my knees, I pulled down his slacks, unbuttoned his shirt. The dark hairs on his chest were flecked with gray. Even his musculature had a distinguished air about it—smooth, defined, not at all bestial like Kyle's somewhat overdeveloped physique.

On all fours, I crawled over him, first indulging my face and lips against his chest, the feathery down like tiny fingers flitting against my skin. With the tip of my tongue running in little curlicues, I made my way slowly down his exquisite stomach to the thicket of his pubic hair, which like his chest, was threaded with gray.

His prick rose slightly to greet my wet, wanting mouth. A

thought crossed my mind: Kyle is an all-you-can-eat buffet; Phillipe is a five-star restaurant. Kyle is an iced cold beer on a hot, Saturday afternoon. Phillipe is a 1945 Margaux. Bic versus Monte Blanc. The Eiffel—

PA: [interrupting] We get it, Ms. Brooks. Please move on.

TRUDIE: Well, variety is the spice—

PA: My patience is running thin.

DA: God is in the details, Counselor.

JAKE: *Agreed. Don't look a gift horse in the mouth, Counselor. Let's not forget, Trudie is revealing very intimate experiences, putting it all out for us to judge. We'll give her the latitude she deserves.*

PA: As you say, Your Honor. Ms. Brooks, you were about to perform fellatio on Phillipe. Let's begin there.

TRUDIE: Certainly. I nestled between his legs before I licked the sleek white droplets at the tip of his cock—a bit salty with just a hint of cumin. I sighed as my mouth crept slowly down his pulsing shaft. One hand grasped the base while my other hand instinctively cupped and gently massaged his tender balls.

Phillipe hummed deeply as his hands cradled my head, guiding me on him so I could provide the distinct pleasure he craved. My tongue strolled languidly as my lips applied just enough pressure. His prick blossomed, filling my mouth as if I were a vase. His simmering sack vibrated against the palm of my hand as I fluttered my fingers, then squeezed, listening to Phillipe's breath and soft moans affirming my touch.

Having this man inside of me, tasting and licking his molten masculinity, and feeling him succumb to my power, my intuitive mastery—all of it filled me with a pleasure I had never known existed until now.

The heat of the fire simmered against my bare ass cheeks,

as if the flames themselves were making love to me. As he grew and stiffened inside of me, he held my head firmly, allowing me to ride him faster, take him in to the very back of my throat. The friction of his prick against my tongue was a feast. Sensations were washing over me, my pussy heating up, my nipples thrumming with sweet pain.

Phillipe's voice emanated from the depths of his gut—not harsh grunts, more like low notes of deep satisfaction. I applied more pressure to his balls and Phillipe spasmed, his hot liquid syrup shooting into my mouth, coating my gums and teeth. I swallowed him as if I'd never eaten before, wanting every last drop inside of me.

As his breathing slowed, I gently released him from my mouth. I rested my head on his groin, his pubic thatch sodden and sweaty, his fingers sliding tenderly through my hair.

"You offered yourself to me so freely, so openly," he whispered. "That is such a gift."

I gazed up at him and met his eyes. My clit cooed, and my hand crept up his stomach to his chest, where I flicked his right nipple.

"Ohhhh," he murmured. His penis stirred beneath me.

I dipped two fingers into my drenched hole and returned to his nipple, slathered it with my juices, then circled and pinched it over and over, feeling it harden against my skin.

What power to feel a spent prick rise to the occasion so quickly.

PA: So this is about power for you?

TRUDIE: When you make a woman come, don't you feel powerful?

PA: Answer my question.

TRUDIE: It seems to me that a man is taking quite a risk to allow a woman to wrap her mouth, lips, and teeth around his dick. He's in the vulnerable position. One strong bite and it's *hasta la vista,* baby! I had the power. I reveled in it. However, I had become a switch-hitter. I'll submit freely and dominate eagerly. Give up control, then seize it.

PA: What happened next?

TRUDIE: He grasped my hand and brought it to his mouth. He licked my scent, sucking my fingers, snaking his tongue around them, between them, gliding his tongue in and out of his mouth, as if he were plying it over my seeping hole.

He guided me up across his body so that my legs straddled his waist. I placed my hands on either side of his head and lowered my breasts to his mouth. The glow from the fire danced across my bare flesh, tiny flames like tongues licking me. Phillipe cupped my breasts in his gorgeous, slender hands, holding them like treasures, and his eyes seemed to swallow them whole. He massaged both, allowing his thumbs to graze softly against my nipples, which rose like small buds of bread dough.

I shimmied my hips and pressed my slick pubes against Phillipe's pelvis, digging into him as if to leave a permanent mark of my cunt against his flesh. From my expanding nipples, a buzzing ache tripped through me down to my clit—hard, swelling, hungry.

PA: Insatiable, wouldn't you say?

TRUDIE: Absolutely. Wildly insatiable. More. More. More.

PA: You have accused yourself of licentiousness—pursuing desires aggressively and selfishly, unchecked by morality, especially in sexual matters. From your testimony, your intimate revelations, I believe you have proved, beyond a reasonable doubt, that you are guilty.

DA: Objection. When did the prosecuting attorney become the judge?

PA: I am only referring to Ms. Brooks's own admission, her own accusation.

JAKE: *Counselor, it is customary in my court to wait until the end of the trial, when I will deliver* my *verdict.*

PA: Sorry, Your Honor.

TRUDIE: Actually, I'm beginning to feel less and less guilt. What's so wrong with pursuing one's desires selfishly and aggressively? I don't accuse myself of licentiousness. I claim it as an accomplishment.

PA: We'll see about that, Ms. Brooks. Continue.

TRUDIE: Okay. So Phillipe was licking my nipples and I groaned when I felt his prick rise, pressing up into the space between my ass cheeks.

He pulled my breasts to his face, his nose and mouth traveling down my cleavage as his thumbs continued to flick against my nipples.

I rose slightly, reached back, clasped my hand around his stiff beauty and lowered myself onto it. My thighs trembled and when I squeezed them, they expressed a sweet soreness—a remnant from my excursion with Kyle on the roof.

As opposed to Kyle's dick rammed inside of me, Phillipe's fit like a glove, and the walls of my happy cunt embraced him wholeheartedly.

He held my right breast in his hands like a bejeweled goblet and circled my flushed areola over and over with his warm, soft tongue, then inserted my nipple between his lips and suckled softly, brilliantly, creating delicious sensations that, again, traveled to my clit.

As I slowly rose and fell upon his cock, I parted the lips of my pussy and began tapping at my slick, erect clit. Phillipe's prick purred and swelled inside of me. I could have stayed in this position with him for hours and hours—not like the fast, furious fucking with Kyle. Phillipe—Rolls-Royce. Kyle—NASCAR.

I released my finger from my clit, wanting to luxuriate in all of the sensations pouring through me. My eyes melded with Phillipe's as his mouth moved to my left tit. I breathed in the scent of us—redolent and lush, like a late spring fog. I clenched my hands on Phillipe's hips as I continued riding him slow and unhurried. He nibbled harder on my nipple, pinching the other between his thumb and index finger. Soft grunts escaped from his mouth, thrummed against my nipple and rippled across my flesh like a stone dropped into a still pond.

I was suddenly seized with the need to put my tongue in his mouth as deeply as possible. I lowered myself, grasped his face, and plunged my tongue between his lips. He met my craving with equal force. I ground my clit against him and all at once, we orgasmed. Our voices cried out, filled each other, fed each other, as our bodies shuddered with melodious spasms.

I collapsed on top of him like a second skin. I woke up an hour later, still there.

PA: I want to refer to a comment you made earlier. I asked if you recalled the words that Kyle had spoken from the script. According to your testimony, and I quote: "Oh, yes, because later that night, on the phone, I helped him with his memorization." Did you mistakenly remember the timing of that phone call?

TRUDIE: No.

PA: So you are saying it is that same evening, and you are with Phillipe?

TRUDIE: Correct. When I woke up, it was about midnight. Phillipe fixed me a tuna sandwich on homemade rosemary foccacia bread. It was quite delicious. Then, I went home. I guess the phone call happened after midnight, so in reality it was the next day, though still that night. Does that make sense?

PA: You returned from having sexual intercourse with Phillipe that night, after having had sexual intercourse with Kyle that day, and you telephoned Kyle?

TRUDIE: Yes. I missed him. I wanted to thank him for the roof.

PA: And he asked you to help him with his lines.

TRUDIE: Yes. We were on the phone for—I don't know, until about three in the morning.

PA: Didn't you have to work the next day?

TRUDIE: Actually, no, this was Friday—I mean, Saturday morning.

PA: Referring to Mr. Cusomono's deposition, page ten, paragraph one, he reports that you engaged in phone sex during this phone call.

TRUDIE: Yes, we did.

PA: I have to say, Ms. Brooks, I'm impressed with your stamina.

TRUDIE: Tell me about it. Usually, my routine was in bed by midnight, up at six.

PA: Who initiated the phone sex?

TRUDIE: Kyle.

PA: Did he say, "Let's have phone sex"?

TRUDIE: No, he said, "I want to lick your asshole."

PA: I want to lick your asshole.

TRUDIE: Stand in line.

PA: Clever, Ms. Brooks. Go on.

TRUDIE: I don't know. It was the way he said it. So innocent, sweet.

PA: Go on.

TRUDIE: He continued: "Baby, please, I want to lick your ass, press my tongue deep into that killer hole. I want you to cry as

I put my fingers inside your wet gash until my whole fist is inside of you, and I'm still lapping at your rear. You're so hot, so consumed, you spread your ass cheeks wide for me, begging me to puncture you with my hunk—"

PA: Hunk?

TRUDIE: Penis. "I want you to weep, baby, weep because it's the most fucking pleasure you've ever known, longed for, dreamed of, and I'm gonna fucking give it all up. Take you over. Make you mine. Tell me, baby, tell me you belong to me."

I could hear him jerking off over the phone. "Your ass belongs to me. Your pussy. Mouth. Tits. Your arms, legs, fingers, toes—all of it belongs to me."

My legs were spread as wide as possible, and I jammed my hand up inside of me while my other hand was smashed against my clit, working it hard. You can't imagine how wet I was—my cunt was dripping, my hot juices slopping out of me. Both of us were grunting like tennis players in sync.

"I'm yours," I screamed. "ALL OF ME!" My hips literally bucked, bounced, rocked. The sound that came out of me shocked the walls of my apartment, shook the bed, echoed out the window. And when Kyle came, forget about it, I had to fling the phone across the room. And I could still hear him—wow!

Once I composed myself, I flung my body to the floor and crawled over to the phone. He was still on the line and we both began laughing, the kind of laugh that makes you cry and need to pee.

Weak. Exhausted. Dazed. Blissed the fuck out. I can't describe it beyond that.

I didn't wake up until two in the afternoon. I've never slept so deeply or soundly.

PA: For the record: Thursday. Friday. Saturday. Four sexual encounters with two men, plus phone sex?

TRUDIE: I guess that's right. It's hard to keep track.

PA: Yes, Ms. Brooks. I agree. When did you begin experiencing difficulties balancing these two relationships?

TRUDIE: That Monday, Phillipe sent me a huge bouquet of white roses, and Kyle made the delivery. Kyle also brought me a single, red rose. He asked who the flowers were from and I lied, said they were from my mother, for my birthday. I didn't like lying to him.

PA: Was it your birthday?

TRUDIE: The next day. Tuesday. So Kyle got all excited and wanted to take me out to dinner Tuesday night. However, Phillipe and I had already planned a date for that night. So, I lied to Kyle again, told him it was tradition that I spend my birthday with my mom.

PA: Did you feel any guilt in deceiving Kyle?

TRUDIE: Yes. I felt awful.

PA: Finally, some sense of morality is present.

DA: Objection!

JAKE: *Sustained. Stick to the facts. Keep your opinions to yourself.*

PA: Sorry, Your Honor. Morality is an issue in this case.

JAKE: *The court will ascertain the role of morality. Is that clear?*

PA: The conventions of our society deem lying immoral.

DA: I disagree. Honesty at all costs can be even more destructive than lying.

JAKE: *Counselors, approach the bench. We are not here to have a philosophical discussion; we are here to adjudicate Ms. Brooks's behavior and the consequences of that behavior to herself and those around her. Let's move on.*

PA: Yes, Your Honor. So, Ms. Brooks, you received flowers from Philippe and Kyle?

TRUDIE: Yes.

PA: Did Kyle leave after the delivery?

TRUDIE: Not right away. I was scheduled for my break so we had a quickie.

PA: Do tell.

TRUDIE: Stockroom. I had the key. I only had fifteen minutes, so we had little time to waste. After our Saturday phone call, I was eager to bend over and let him have a go. In fact, that's all I had thought about.

PA: Sodomy?

TRUDIE: In some states sodomy refers to oral sex as well as anal activity.

PA: I don't need a legal education.

TRUDIE: I'm hungry for knowledge myself. Well, I locked the door behind us, pulled up my skirt, bent over a stack of boxes, and demanded, "Give it to me. Now."

Kyle had a tube of lube in his pocket. He pulled it out, along with a condom. Of course, since my pussy was on overdrive, I was already creaming. I had also stopped wearing panties. There is something very tantalizing about crossing your legs and squeezing your thighs tight while you're answering the phone, saying over and over, "Denom, Dillon, and Tate. How may I direct your call?" You just keep squeezing, and eventually, you can give yourself an orgasm.

PA: At the office? While you are being paid? Do you consider that responsible?

TRUDIE: Hey, it didn't stop me from answering the phone; in fact, I was more polite, even chipper.

PA: Let's return to the stockroom.

TRUDIE: My breasts were crushed against the boxes. From behind, Kyle cupped my throbbing pussy, slathering his fingers in the warm rain between my legs. Slowly, agonizingly, teasingly, he traced a trail along the highway between my holes. I grabbed my ass cheeks, spread them wide, as wide as possible, digging my own nails into my skin.

He soaked me with my silken cream, his fingers expertly rimming my ass, sneaking in, quickly exiting, making me fierce, raw, my need expanding beyond reason. I heard the sound of his teeth ripping open the condom package.

He grunted as he slipped it over his gigantic hunk, continuing to play my hot hole.

"Please, please," I begged, "give it to me, Kyle. Fuck me. You've got to fuck me!"

I could feel the tip of his rod press against me, stretching me inch by inch. He actually was being too careful. I reached back, grabbed his ass cheeks, and shoved him inside of me in one glorious swoop.

An indescribable pain ripped through me—a collision of ecstasy and violence. He thrust at me frantically, now knowing how I needed it.

"Fuck, Trudie, goddamn it, you beautiful, amazing bitch!" He held my hips firmly, grinding and slamming into me.

My own fingers careened to my drenched slit, and I spanked my clit, slapped her mercilessly—punishing and pleasing myself at the same time.

As if on cue, Kyle's palm delivered a shocking sting to my ass cheek.

I cried out, "Oh, yes! Do it! Drum me, Kyle!"

With both hands, he let me have it. I was a bongo being beaten. The slaps bounced off the concrete walls. All at once, Kyle surged into me, brutal, vicious, and his steaming seed torpedoed inside my ass.

Amazingly, he didn't stop slamming away at my aching cheeks, and in a frenzied, cataclysmic explosion, I came. I shoved my fist in my mouth, muting the scream that blasted out from the depths of my throbbing groin.

Our breathing was ragged and deep. His arms were wrapped around me tightly from behind, his face nuzzled against my neck, and he whispered, "Baby, I love you. I love you. I . . ."

PA: Do you need a Kleenex, Ms. Brooks?

TRUDIE: Please.

PA: Are you sad because Kyle declared that he loved you, not knowing that you were also seeing another man?

TRUDIE: No. I'm crying because it was such a beautiful, tender moment.

PA: What happened next?

TRUDIE: I went back to my desk. Kyle left and we made a date to go out Wednesday night for my birthday.

PA: Is it your opinion that your sex with Kyle in the stockroom was punishing because you were guilty of lying and wanted to be punished?

TRUDIE: That's a very simplistic assessment of my motivation. There are so many layers to sexual expression—history, dreams, fantasies, exploration, discovery, testing and pushing boundaries, playing roles, emotional realities, love, hate—I mean, I could go on and on. I don't think it's this or that. I think sex can embody a whole universe of possibility. But at this point, I'd say, I began to feel like I was spinning.

PA: Can you clarify, please?

TRUDIE: Phone calls, all day Monday. From Phillipe. From Kyle. "After the bar exam I want to take you to the south of France." "Hey, when you're done with that test, it's you, me, and a motorcycle ride to Baja." "I have tickets to the opera Saturday night; I'd like you to join me." "Babe, Tom Petty, Staples Center, this Saturday. We're there!"

In fact, Kyle came back Monday late afternoon to make another delivery, and I walked him to the elevator just as Phillipe stepped out. I freaked, blurted out that I had to pee, and made a beeline to the restroom.

PA: Was Phillipe there for business or pleasure?

TRUDIE: Both. After his meeting, he was taking me to an expensive boutique in Beverly Hills. He wanted to buy me a dress for that evening. I was going to be meeting some of his friends and he wanted to show me off. I realized I was in a little over my head. Way over.

PA: In what way?

TRUDIE: I wanted to please Phillipe, but I had a gnawing feeling that I was a runaway train about to derail. Maybe I was having too much sex. In the boutique, I found myself feeling irritable. Thank God the saleswoman offered me champagne, because I had this impulsive urge to bolt. It was suddenly all too much: south of France. Baja. Opera. Tom Petty. Lying about the flowers, my birthday. I drank too much bubbly. And, later, at the dinner, I indulged in more. It wasn't pretty.

PA: Can you describe what happened at the dinner?

TRUDIE: [sighs] I was seated next to a beautiful, African-American woman who told me that Phillipe had talked a lot about me.

PA: For the record, I have a deposition from the woman in question, Angela Adams. Ms. Adams states that you appeared "drunk and agitated."

TRUDIE: That's correct. She knew I was studying for the bar, and I told her I felt a little sidetracked.

"Sidetracked? By whom? Phillipe?" she asked.

"No," I said. "By choices I've made recently."

"I don't understand," she said.

I was pretty much gulping the champagne as if it were lemonade. I started rambling: "Who knows why I got sidetracked—who knows? Who knows why I'm sitting here in a red dress that I despise. Who knows why I didn't say no when he bought it for me, but I didn't. I don't know. If someone said, 'Do you want to fuck in an elevator?' I'd probably say YES. I mean, suddenly, NO is becoming YES. My whole life was a NO, and now it's a fucking YES!"

I was so carried away that I didn't realize everyone had stopped talking, and they were focused on me. Phillipe came up, took my arm, and I flipped out. I just kept repeating: "No. No. No. No. No."

As you can imagine, Phillipe was completely taken aback. I was horrified, and I ran out of his house. I guess I didn't make a very good impression on his friends.

PA: Drinking irresponsibly. Behaving recklessly. Psychological distress. Public humiliation. Is it fair to say that your world was falling apart?

TRUDIE: Sometimes things have to fall apart in order to change, truly change.

PA: Wouldn't it be fair to say you were wreaking havoc on others and yourself?

TRUDIE: That would be fair.

PA: In fact, you displayed absolute disregard for Phillipe's well being?

TRUDIE: Yes, I did.

PA: You were selfish. Out of control. Negligent. Dishonest. Do you agree?

TRUDIE: I do. Yes.

PA: And after you ran out of Phillipe's house, what did you do?

TRUDIE: I went to see Kyle.

PA: You went to see Kyle? My God, Ms. Brooks, have you no decency?

DA: Objection. Counsel is being overly dramatic.

JAKE: *Sustained. Lose the theatrics.*

TRUDIE: I couldn't bear to go home. I knew Phillipe would try to call, maybe come over. He'd never seen me act so strangely before. I just couldn't face him. I was humiliated.

JAKE: *Let's reconvene in a half hour.*

JAKE

I can't help but think about Alex—our last year, when she was having her affair and I didn't realize it. She would be agitated one moment, clingy and needy the next. Her drinking increased. She was confused, guilty, and obsessed. Torn by her desires. Finally, she derailed her own life by completely eliminating it.

Had a part of me known that she was betraying me? Did I just turn a blind eye to her distress, her crisis, because I didn't want it to be true?

Although her circumstances are different, Trudie is offering me a gift, insight into Alex's pain, her private nightmare. I'd like to meet her—I think she'd have the capacity and empathy to hear my story, maybe bring me some relief.

JAKE: *All right, Trudie, please take the stand.*

PA: So, you went to see Kyle?

TRUDIE: Yes. I knew he had an acting class in Hollywood that would be over soon. So I took a cab and waited outside for him.

I stood on the sidewalk watching humanity streaming past me—all colors, shapes, and sizes, in such a remarkable variety of pairings. How many secrets did they carry? How many of them longed to be with someone else? How do we make that choice? For some, it's only one choice in their lifetimes; for others, they choose a succession of many lovers. Who can carry off having more than one lover at the same time? Is it ever easy and uncomplicated?

The students spilled out of the building. Kyle was last, and when he saw me, his face lit up like the lights of Las Vegas. A beam of that light shot through me, and even though I was still feeling the effects of the champagne, I jumped into his arms.

"Damn, girl," he said. "You're like Cinderella at the ball in that dress. Like fucking royalty. Where you been?"

"At a dinner party. I left early." At least that was the truth.

He grabbed my hand, pulled me back into the building. It was a dingy space with a stage at one end and dozens of metal chairs facing it. He called out to a tall Hispanic man who was onstage stretching. "Hey, Gonzalo, I'll lock up tonight, dude."

Still holding my hand, he guided me behind the stage where a room was crammed with dressing tables covered with makeup. Along the walls there were racks and racks of costumes. Old Playbills, headshots, and flyers were tacked everywhere.

"Take off your dress and let's play," he said with a smile.

That was exactly what I needed—playtime. I happily stripped off the red dress and stood before Kyle in my stilettos, bra, garter, and stockings. He undressed, too. I had no idea what he had in mind.

"I've been fucking high all day after the storage closet," he said, his smile continuing to shoot rays of light into my darkness. "Take everything off," he instructed.

As I did, he pulled out two costumes. "They're doing a rendition of Pocahontas, but with guys playing all the characters. I want the lead."

He handed me a costume, a period man's uniform, circa the Civil War.

"You're playing the dude Poca falls for, Captain what's his name. I haven't read the script yet, but I thought I could do some memory associations. Who knows, I might have been a knockout squaw in a past life."

He put on the female Native American costume, a soft, tan, beaded suede dress, with leather strips and feathers. I put on my blue period uniform, tucked my hair up and put on my hat.

"Okay," Kyle said, "give me a little face paint."

He sat before a mirror, and I riffled through the cosmetics, picking up blushes and eye shadow and using them to draw lines on Kyle's exquisitely adorable face.

PA: Ms. Brooks, let me interrupt. You were now playing dress up with Kyle not one hour after your abysmal behavior at Phillipe's?

TRUDIE: I wasn't thinking about Phillipe. I was wrapped up in Kyle's childlike spirit, carried along by it, enjoying myself.

PA: Sociopaths are often associated with a lack of conscience.

TRUDIE: I HAD A HARD FUCKING DAY!

PA: The witness is being hostile!

JAKE: *Can you blame her?*

PA: One man happily fucked you in the behind. Another man bought you a $2,000 outfit, and you metaphorically spat in his face. Now you're playing in the sandbox with Kyle!

DA: Objection. Counsel is badgering the witness and putting words in her mouth.

JAKE: *I'm curious, Trudie, about your ability to turn off what had just happened with Phillipe and enter another reality with Kyle so completely.*

TRUDIE: I know. I agree. I had never had this experience before. Kyle. Phillipe. Phillipe. Kyle. It's as if they appealed to separate parts of myself. As if the two of them formed the perfect lover—just like that.

JAKE: *I'm going to sustain the objection and remind Counsel to resist the urge to condemn Ms. Brooks's behavior.*

PA: Continue with your recollection of the events.

TRUDIE: Kyle had divinely, almost oddly, soft skin. I later learned he moisturized several times a day. Actors, right? So I applied a hint of lipstick on him—the color was called Coral Sea, and I swear he really looked like a woman, a bit butch, but lovely, really lovely.

We went out to the stage. He set up a single spotlight and brought out a pole, logs for a pretend bonfire, a rubber knife for me, and a whip made of dried reeds.

Kyle then decided I would be playing the part of the evil officer who captures Pocahontas, ties her up, and tortures her.

Separated from her tribe, Poca sat alone in the woods keeping warm by the bonfire, communicating with the moon, the breeze, the earth, and the hidden creatures surrounding her.

I called my character Captain Marquis—after the Marquis de Sade. Captain Marquis was a real sadistic bastard who particularly despised the Red Man.

"Hoo hoo." Kyle made the sound of a night owl. *"Hoo hoo."*

He sat cross-legged in front of the bonfire. Behind him, I crept up, brandishing my sharp knife. I swung my arm around his neck from behind, pressing the blade against his throat.

"Look what I've got," I sneered. "A red whore all to myself."

Kyle struggled to free himself from my grip, but only in the manner of a woman who is physically helpless against a strong man.

I ripped one of the leather strips from his costume and tied his wrists together. I forced him to his feet. His eyes were wide, fearful, expressing the palpable terror of a female at the mercy of an evil man. I shoved him toward the pole and secured him to it face forward. I tore another leather strip and blindfolded him.

I pressed my lips to his ear, murmuring low and deep, "You are nothing but an animal to me. One worthy of being slaughtered, roasted, and eaten."

"Please," Kyle begged in a high-pitched voice, "don't kill me!"

I circled the pole menacingly, then delivered a tentative slap across his face. Kyle, in his own voice, whispered: "Show no mercy, baby. I can take it. It's Method Acting."

I slapped him harder, feeling the sting against my palm. "I'm not going to kill you, you filthy worm. I'm going to make you beg me for death."

Poca tried to spit in my face—though he couldn't see it through the blindfold. "My land, my people—the moon and stars as my witnesses—will see to it that you will exact no punishment that will not come back to you a hundred-fold."

I shoved my hand up under his dress, clutched his package, squeezed. He moaned.

"Your people?" I taunted. "You are not even human. You are bile, less than the cockroach that will feast upon your worthless carcass."

PA: Your portrayal of evil is very convincing, Ms. Brooks. Perhaps too convincing.

TRUDIE: It's the repression of rage and dark impulses that gives birth to true evil, Counselor. Kyle gave me an outlet to express aspects of myself I'd never expressed. I believe it's called human nature.

PA: So now you're an expert in psychology?

TRUDIE: I did get my bachelor's degree in behavioral psychology, so I'm not wholly uninformed.

PA: I see. Please go on.

TRUDIE: Clutching his hair, I jerked his neck back, then spat in his face. "You're the excrement of a pig." His cock stiffened in my grasp.

Anger flourished in Poca's voice: "The Great Spirit will choke you with your own stinking shit."

I tugged his hunk hard. He yelped, surprised, then revealed a hint of a smile, urging me to go on.

I ripped off his costume from behind—easily, because it was fastened with Velcro.

"Father Wind protects me," he continued. "Each blow you deliver is but a feather on my flesh."

"Slutty, stinking squaw!" I walloped his right ass cheek.

He flinched, gritted his teeth.

He stood before me naked, a man/woman exposed, his ass cheeks clenched, his thighs, massive as tree trunks, trembled as if pounded by a frantic wind. He/she was so vulnerable, so completely under my control.

My clit quivered at the sight. From behind, I reached my

hands to his chest, pinched his nipples, pulling at them like rubber bands.

"Owww," Poca cried.

I remembered seeing this movie, I think it was *Little Big Man*, in which the Native American men had a ritual of piercing, then hanging from, their own nipples. It was equally horrifying and mesmerizing—stretching their nipples beyond comprehension, absorbing then transcending the agonizing pain.

"You little savages with your putrid milk," I seethed as I twisted, squashed, punished his hardening nubs over and over. His body jerked in response, his cock sprang up.

I laughed, released my hands, then spit again. My saliva landed at the top of his crack, then dripped down between his cheeks like a tiny waterfall.

Breathing hard, Kyle muttered, "The spirit of the reeds you flog me with will find you in your dreams, wrap around your throat, and steal your breath away."

I broke character: "You want me to whip you?"

"Oh, yeah, baby. Let's go!" Kyle answered.

Had I not been acting, I'm not sure if I could actually bring myself to whip anyone, even if he wanted it. But, I will admit, the thought of it aroused me—the quivering in my clit spread to the sodden cavern inside, and even my precious asshole joined by pulsing slightly.

Maybe I should chuck law school and go into acting. It is so freeing to have permission to be anything you can imagine.

First, I loosened the leather tie around his wrists so he could slide to his knees, then I tightened the restraints even more. I picked up the dried reed whip and held it in my grip, feeling a sense of tremendous power surge through my body.

I brushed it lightly against his ass cheeks—it made a whooshing, rattling noise.

"Shit, squaw, you are in for it!" I cried. I reared back my arm and whacked his flesh with an unforgiving blow.

He bucked, screamed. The whip left a map of red welts on his sweet ass cheeks. Instead of hesitating or feeling scared that I was going too far, I felt the sheer charge of adrenaline that coursed through me take over, propelling my arm to deliver another blow—fierce, exacting, unequivocal.

He grunted as his hunk stiffened and rose. "No, no more!" Then he turned in my direction and grinned.

The reed whispered against his thighs, shimmied against his ass. I swept it across his muscled back, whisked the whip tenderly against his skin.

My sudden gentleness caused Kyle to moan deeply. I then lashed his ass again, then again. The strength in my arm seemed to grow with each blow. The map of welts was now incomprehensible, trail upon trail of chaotic wounds.

"Oh, fuck, baby. I'm so fucking ready!" he cried out.

I yanked his arm and twisted him around to face me. His cock was aimed like a tomahawk toward me as if luring me to willingly be split open.

I unbuttoned the pants of my uniform and let them slide down my thighs to the floor. Then I slipped off my shoes, and stepped out of them. I jerked off his blindfold, parted my legs, and stood in front of Kyle, taunting him with my tantalizing, steaming pussy. I gyrated my hips while brushing the reeds through my trimmed grasses.

I stepped close to him, straddling his waist, but keeping my cunt just out of reach of his gaping mouth.

"Where's your Great Spirit now, Red Bitch?" I sneered. I swept the reed against his thickening dick.

"Uhhh," he grunted.

"Turn away from me!" I yelled.

Still on his knees, he twisted back to face the pole. I knelt quietly on all fours and began to lap at the wounds I had caused, feeling the heat of his skin against my hungry tongue.

His moans filled the stage and the theater, his sounds mixed with my own voice as I soothed him like a mommy attending to a child's scraped knee. Shushing, licking, I turned and lowered myself to my back, then slid between his legs so that my face was directly below his engorged shaft. His swollen balls hung like huge teardrops and my tongue plied them first, my mouth stretched wide. I took the furry jewels in, sucking and thrashing my tongue against them.

"Oh. Oh. Oh. Oh." Kyle's voice, deep and ragged, filled me with a resolve to luxuriate, always, in the symphony of the flesh, the overwhelming purity of pleasuring another, and in so doing, pleasuring oneself.

Simmering saliva dripped down my chin, and I used it to coat my fingers. Then I reached up and began to stroke Kyle's masculine trophy as my tongue slithered like a snake against his balls, which pulsed like small balloons filling with hot water.

He rocked his hips as my hand polished his pride, rubbing the pulsing shaft faster and faster, feeling his thighs trembling. Then I pressed my lips tight around his right ball. It vibrated, about to burst, and Kyle's whole body shuddered as if he were the Serengeti and a stampede of beasts charged across his terrain. His liquid stream spurted forth. I slid out from beneath him, sat up, and wrapped my arms tightly around his broad back, absorbing the spasms that careened through his being.

A few moments passed, and finally my hands trailed down his arms to his wrists as I released him from captivity.

He collapsed onto his back, completely spent, wrung out, but with enough energy to keep a smile fixed on his face. I curled up against him, my face resting on his chest, and we fell asleep under the spotlight moon, on a mostly empty stage.

As it turned out, the young squaw, Pocahontas, didn't need to be rescued after all.

DA: Trudie, I just want to thank you for your candor. I'm very moved.

TRUDIE: You're welcome.

PA: Moved by her story? Well, Counsel, now *your* character is in question.

JAKE: *That's enough, gentlemen.*

PA: Frankly, Ms. Brooks, I'm flabbergasted. You spurned Phillipe, humiliated yourself—and him—in front of his friends, and then went to Kyle to act out a ridiculous scenario involving cross-dressing, sadism, and violence. How would you imagine a jury of your peers would judge you in this moment?

DA: Objection, Your Honor, this isn't a jury trial.

JAKE: *Overruled. Answer the question.*

TRUDIE: Your Honor, I hope with compassion and empathy. I'm just a woman, going through an experience that caught me off-guard, but one that might be essential to my living fully. Carpe diem, seize the day, and all that.

PA: In your case I would say, "carpe dick."

JAKE: *Strike that. You're tiring me, Counselor. . . .*

PA: Withdrawn. [Sighs.] I believe we have arrived at your birthday.

TRUDIE: Yes. Tuesday. I turned twenty-six. We didn't wake up until morning, and Kyle took me to the House of Pancakes for my birthday breakfast. Luckily, I had a change of clothes in the car. I showed up at the office a little late, maybe an hour, but it was my special day, so nobody minded. There was a delivery waiting for me, a blue box from Tiffany & Co., a gift from Phillipe with a note.

PA: I'd like to enter this note as exhibit A. I have a copy here. Would you read to the court what Phillipe wrote?

TRUDIE: "My beauty, I apologize for not noting your distress, even before the dinner party began. I often mistake my desires, my wishes, for others'. Had I paid attention, I would have realized you were uncomfortable in the red dress and not up for meeting my friends so quickly after our meeting. Forgive me. It is your birthday, and I hope you still desire to spend the evening with me. Yours, Phillipe."

PA: And the gift?

TRUDIE: A sterling silver bracelet embedded with tiny diamonds, like stars. It was breathtaking.

PA: How did you feel about the note?

TRUDIE: I appreciated his looking deeper than the superficiality of my irrational behavior and realizing I was on the edge and overwhelmed. It doesn't excuse what I did, and I intended to make it up to him. We all make mistakes.

PA: Did the note lead you to feel any remorse for having gone to Kyle and having sexual relations with him?

TRUDIE: Not really. There is absolutely no way to sit across from Kyle with whipped cream on his nose and that fucking smile plastered on his face as he hoovers down an enormous pile of chocolate chip pancakes and not feel simply happy to be alive.

In fact, the bracelet, although stunning, didn't make me feel the same level of joy. The note, though, filled me with tenderness toward Phillipe, and I longed to be with him again.

PA: So did you contact Phillipe?

TRUDIE: Yes, I messengered a personal note to him: "For my birthday, I'll be wearing only your gift."

PA: What were the plans you had with Phillipe?

TRUDIE: He was cooking me a surprise dinner. I arrived at his house at eight o'clock, as scheduled, wearing a black trench coat, with nothing on underneath, except the bracelet on my wrist—and high heels, of course.

PA: What was your state of mind?

TRUDIE: Excited. Nervous. Shy. He opened the door, and I said, "I'm so—"

He cut me off, pressed a finger to my lips. "Not a word about it," he said. He took my hand, guided me inside. I dropped my coat immediately, felt a flush of sensual excitement trickle down my spine as his eyes drifted across my body as if caressing me with thousands of fingers.

I was startled when a woman appeared from the kitchen. She was wearing a tiny black dress, covered only by an even tinier white apron. Tall, blond, with impossibly long legs, and a porcelain face coveted by angels, she said, "Hello, Trudie. Happy birthday! I'm Inga, and I'll be serving you this evening. May I get you something to drink?"

She didn't react at all to my being naked. In fact, she seemed pleased, even titillated by my exposed presence.

Feeling a bit taken aback, I requested something a little stronger than wine, a vodka on the rocks. I hoped it would help equip me to accommodate the reality of her unexpected presence in our evening together.

She disappeared into the kitchen. I heard the sound of ice cubes tumbling into a glass. Phillipe smiled and wrapped his arm around my waist.

"I hope you don't mind. She's very special—makes any evening unforgettable," he said.

"Not at all," I replied, wanting to be open, agreeable, and make up for my horrid behavior the night before. I turned to him. "You won't let me apologize."

"No need, beauty," he whispered. "I want to thank you for your honesty, for being completely free in the moment to reveal yourself, even to strangers. That takes a lot of courage."

"I felt like such a coward, running away."

"Quite the opposite," he said. "You took care of yourself, did not fall into the trap of social pretensions. Brava."

Oh God, what a soul this man had, I thought. So open, so forgiving, such wisdom and compassion.

He continued: "I often fall into the trap of wanting to control and orchestrate an evening, to not be open to chaos and unpredictability. You taught me an important lesson. I did try to call you. Where did you go?"

I stiffened, slightly. "To a friend's," I replied.

"Perfect," he said, as his knowing hand caressed my back, slid to my ass, then led me to sit on the chair by the blazing fire.

Inga reappeared with my drink and a plate of escargot, one of my favorite delicacies. She slipped a white linen napkin onto my bare lap, handed me my drink, then picked up one of the garlic-scented snails and held it to my waiting lips. My throat heated, hungering to swallow the delicious morsel whole. As I did, an unexpected moan escaped from my lips.

"You are even more beautiful than I imagined," Inga said.

"I couldn't imagine the extent of your irresistibility, even though Phillipe went to great lengths describing you to me."

Phillipe sat across from me sipping a martini, drinking in the scene before him: two women, one naked, the other serving her. It was obvious that he was completely filled with satisfaction.

"Another?" Inga asked, holding up another morsel for me to devour. I parted my lips and sucked it in greedily. Then I took a sip of my own drink.

"Inga," I blurted impulsively, "would you be willing to give me a birthday gift?"

"Of course," she cooed. "I'm here at your command."

My eyes embraced Phillipe's curious, enticing gaze.

"I love Phillipe, in a way I can hardly comprehend," I explained. "And I acted so badly the other night, I want to make it up to him. On my birthday, all I want is to give him a gift he'll never forget."

Inga knelt before me, placing her hands on my knees. "Anything, lovely one, anything at all."

"Phillipe," I whispered. "Unzip your pants. Release that miracle between your legs."

He complied without hesitation. He pulled out his elegant prick—stiffening by the second.

"Inga," I continued, "what would you like to do with him?"

Her hands were still on my knees, and she squeezed my flesh, her eyes seducing me, drawing me into the angelic haze that surrounded her.

"Tell me what you want," she answered.

"Kiss me," I commanded.

We both leaned forward, and our lips met for a brief, momentous moment. Then I whispered, "Take his cock into your mouth, and treat the moment as if it were your last opportunity to have a man inside of you, in this most unique way."

She smiled at me, her eyes communicating complete understanding. I resisted reaching out to touch her breasts—perfectly shaped mounds that begged to be devoured.

I returned my attention to Phillipe, whose gaze was fixed on us: two women sharing a kiss and whispered secrets. His prick responded in kind, rising to the occasion.

Inga rose, moved to Phillipe, and knelt in front of him. I got up and sauntered behind Phillipe's chair as Inga clasped her hand around the base of his shaft and slowly, deliberately grazed her tongue down the length of him. Phillipe sighed.

I bent down and whispered in his ear, "Happy birthday to me, baby."

I watched as she ministered to his rising cock, her technique so individual, the way she cupped his balls and rocked them slowly back and forth like a cradle as she sucked, gentle and devouring all at once.

I dipped my hands beneath his shirt and began to massage his chest, gliding my palms over his growing nipples. I leaned down, my lips against his ear, and I began to tell him everything I wanted to say about my experiences with him: "Phillipe, your wanting me, having me, loving me, understanding and forgiving me, you are a man like no other. So powerful and gentle, so mysterious and open. My cunt aches when I'm not with you. I awake from dreams, feeling all of you inside of me, taking me, melting my flesh, my emotions, allowing me to shudder and scream. Beautiful, strong, fucking graceful man, you have given me everything. Just tell me that you want me."

He groaned. "Ohhhh, I want you."

Our tongues met, sucking and wet. The soft moans emanated from Inga's lips that were completely encased around Phillipe's prick, her mouth glided like a speed skater, up and down, effortlessly and smooth.

He wrapped his lips around my tongue and pulled it into his mouth with a ferocity I hadn't experienced, so hard my tongue felt a pang of sweet pain. I wanted him to devour it like I had the escargot.

All at once a punch of hot breath hit my mouth as his body jerked, and he shot his sweet jissum into Inga's mouth. I breathed in his harsh breath, pulling it deep into my gut, wanting to feel the essence of his life force enter me completely.

Inga used a napkin to wipe Phillipe's cock and her mouth. She zipped him up, then rose to finish the preparations for dinner.

"Thank you, Trudie," she said, patting my shoulder before she disappeared back into the kitchen.

"Thank you," I murmured.

I sat at Phillipe's feet, fully naked, nestling my face in his groin, allowing the scent of his sex to permeate my senses. I wasn't even hungry for dinner; I felt completely sated, happy, and so alive to be planted between the legs of this generous, transcendent man.

PA: So, Ms. Brooks, we've come to the end.

TRUDIE: Not quite. I went home that night—alone, for the record—and realized in order for me to continue I had to make a decision.

PA: Between Phillipe and Kyle?

TRUDIE: Not quite.

PA: Please, we're waiting with bated breath to hear what you have to say.

TRUDIE: The next day I went to the office, entered the elevator, and just as the doors were about to close, two men called out: "Hold the door." As you have probably surmised, it was Phillipe *and* Kyle. They both moved to either side of me and I introduced them to each other. I had no choice but to do it, as it was obvious they both knew *me.*

I finally confessed that I'd been seeing them both. They were shocked, of course. I told them that I loved them both enormously, but it'd become too confusing. I needed to take a break and get back to my studies.

PA: So, you were finally honest. Do you feel that exonerates you from your actions?

TRUDIE: Not completely. I did betray them both. I was dishonest. Negligent in how I handled them emotionally. But if I had to do it over again, I probably wouldn't change a thing. You trip and fall, get up, keep walking, but you can be sure, you'll trip again.

PA: Your Honor, the prosecution rests.

JAKE: *Would the defense care to cross-examine the witness?*

DA: No, your Honor, we're satisfied with Ms. Brooks's testimony.

JAKE: *I believe I'm ready to deliver my ruling. In the matter of Trudie Brooks, plaintiff, versus Trudie Brooks, defendant, the court finds you guilty of being human, of admitting your flaws and mistakes, of taking risks, freeing yourself of your limitations, and of recklessly, negligently, dishonestly, passionately, and fully embracing the darkness and light of living life. We wish you well.*

Case closed.

Well, Red Shoes, I hope you didn't find my trial boring or too self-indulgent. If you've reached the end of this letter, I can only hope that you've understood what I now know: that life can turn on a dime. Maybe the true test of living is to take those turns, follow where they lead, and learn. Maybe this is presumptuous, but I think something must have happened in your life that sent you in a direction that you never expected, just like that. Just maybe you're trying, as I am, to learn. I wish you well. Thanks for listening.

JAKE

So how did I do, Stella? Was I fair, impartial? Too lenient? You want to watch reruns of Law & Order? *How about we hit the beach first, participate in this thing called living life. What do you say, Stella? Want to chase a stick? That's my girl.*

Another Woman's Lipstick

◆

JAKE

Hey Stella, enough with the sea and the surf, eh? Three days of beaching it and I'm still trying to get the sand out of my ears. You, on the other hand, have proven that you are the reigning Queen of Fetch. Me, I have to tell you, I missed my relationship—the one with my P.O. Box, I mean.

Listen, my canine wonder, I know you never forget a smell, but do you remember all of our conversations, too? How about the one early this morning when I told you to wait outside the coffee shop while I got my mail? Nothing unusual about that, but I did kid you not to talk to strangers. Something told me that we needed to be out in the world, in the fresh air and all that, for what was coming our way. And I did not mean the next train. . . .

Listen to this:

♦ ♦ ♦

Dear Red Shoes,

To get fucked is everything. To really get fucked means you give everything, every part of yourself, the depth of your being with each touch, stroke, feeling. All of you is naked, teased open, visible to the hungry eye of whomever wants you or imagines wanting you. Yet is it *you* they want? Or is it feeling itself, wanting to fuck you to feel their own existence? Maybe you can make them feel what they think they're making you feel. And what the fuck would that be? That you would be willing to spread your legs as wide as you could, that you would expose your flesh and part yourself, offer all of your desire, maybe even share a handful of secrets after they've made you come, and you're open to wanting more, expressing more, demanding more.

And you would say: Fuck me. Faster. Deeper. Slower. Now. Make me kneel, and twist my nipples while you pump me with your fingers, the palm of your hand slapping my sweet meat with each stroke. That's right. Make me give myself to you. With your hands. Make me surrender. With your tongue. Insist that I let you in deeper. With your passion. Make me bend over. Soothe me with your intention. Make every touch seem swaddled in a majestic velvet that feels like I've been touched by nature itself. Make me know that this moment could not feel any sweeter. That my life, in this moment, *is* this moment. That it is more than perfect. That it is, perhaps, complete.

And that our love, way beyond the tonguing, throbbing, pumping of sex, is even more severe.

I had that kind of love with my husband.
    Until *her*.

It would have to be red, wouldn't it? That was what she was wearing the first time I saw her: red lipstick. My face is burning, raw with emotion as I write this. But I'm getting ahead of myself. . . .

We'd been together forever. From when we were eleven years old, anyway. Zoey and Robert . . . Robert and Zoey . . . You know that old childhood rhyme: *Me and you sitting in a tree, k-i-s-s-i-n-g. . . .?* That really was us, kissing in the cleft of a maple, and that really was us later on, complete with the marriage. We stopped short of the baby carriage, though, because our careers were just gaining momentum when we finally got engaged after college, during our early twenties. A few years passed, and once we'd climbed a mountain of hard work, both of our careers flourished. I was a clothing designer; Robert was a builder.

We were successful, sought after. If you told us what you wanted, we designed it. And *we* were it—what everybody seemed to want, the couple everyone envied. My eyes. His smile. Not only were we perfect together in public, Robert was a transcendent lover and a gifted chef, and I had a bottomless appetite for each. I loved spicy food, how we craved each other's scent, and that our favorite number was sixty-nine.

Of the many wonders that I loved about us, I cherished that we were still spontaneous. Though we'd been each other's everything for eons, we never stopped yearning to ignite life anew at any moment. So it only revved me up when he tossed a pillow at me that morning in the bedroom. The look on his face reminded me of the boy he still was, the long-haired boy I'd loved from the first moment I saw him on the yellow school bus so long ago.

I caught the pillow and pretended to fluff it up as an adult would before placing it back on the freshly made white bed. Then I whirled around and slammed it into his chest.

War!

Wrestling for control, he pinned me against the four-posted bed in a few delightful seconds. His mouth covered mine as entirely as the rest of his body suddenly did, his butter-brown trench coat draped over us like an unintended shield against the outside world. Longing bloomed in our kiss as we rolled around, the pillow our pawn as our tongues plunged into scrumptious battle, until the grown-up Robert finally disentangled himself.

"I gotta go," he announced. His wheat-colored ponytail was still presentable. His round, gold-rimmed glasses gleamed undisturbed. My Mr. Cool.

"Then go," I said simply. I could be cool, too.

"You know I love you," he said.

"More than anything," I replied.

"That's my line," he went on.

"But it's my heart you're talking about," I challenged.

"And mine, angel. It's all yours. You still want me?"

"More than ever."

His lips found mine again, our tongues slow and deep. Our bodies curled into each other's as they had countless times. Parts of me went soft, seeming softer still against the hardening parts of him.

"It's not fair. . . . It's just not fair. . . . " he whined.

Ah, my Mr. Not So Cool. I tossed the pillow to the bed and leapt up, the adult now. "You're the one who's gotta go. Just go!"

He left with a chagrined smile as I lay down once more. I sank into the cloud-soft pillows, thinking how idyllic my life was, how ideal our relationship was, how supremely love had embraced my deepest being. I lay there with my perfect thoughts, our rapture, expecting much, much more.

It was only after I got up that my world fell apart.

· · ·

Take a guess, Red Shoes. Where does a woman find what she dreads most? I'll give you a hint: They say most car accidents take place within three miles of one's home. I'd wager that most intimate accidents take place *inside* one's home. A motel receipt upended in his wallet, maybe. Or a clandestine dinner backing into his credit card. Possibly the crash of another woman's lips against his otherwise pristine white collar.

In the bathroom, I lifted Robert's white Oxford from the laundry hamper with two fingers. The odor was what had drawn me to it: like new buds in early spring. Delicate yet full of promise. As I inhaled the scent, my heart retreated under my ribs.

I'm sad to say it all started with a cliché. You guessed it: another woman's scent. Another woman's lipstick.

Red, of course. And as if it were blood, the sight of it sickened me. I fell back against the wall, staring at the stain. I was hypnotized by my own shock, by Robert's unimaginable betrayal, and I slid to the bathroom floor, landing on my knees.

I have no idea how long I stayed like that, as if I were behind an impenetrable barrier. I heard the ringing of the house phone, the increasingly insistent beeping of my cell phone, letting me know that messages had been left on its voice-mail system, and the sound outside of an occasional passing car. But I couldn't bring myself to rise.

It had been morning, bright, new, possible, but now I lay curled in the shadows, my knees sore, my back an aching steel rod. I had missed an entire day at work. As night fell, I dragged myself back to the bed. How much time passed, I don't know. Eventually, I heard the front door open. Paralyzed, I could not move.

It was Robert. His footsteps. I finally opened my eyes as he took off his coat and approached the bed. He crouched down before me.

"Are you okay?" he asked.

His voice. My mind suddenly flashed with images of us racing around the bed earlier. "Uh huh," I managed.

"I called you all day long," he went on.

I didn't respond.

He leaned in close. "You smell good," he said.

I stiffened. Was it *her* he smelled on me?

"Have you eaten?" he asked.

I shook my head slowly.

"I'll get you some soup," he said.

I saw only us, him pinning me from above, the urgent way we'd kissed earlier.

"You want some soup?" Uncertainty had surfaced in his voice.

"Sure," I answered. Just to get him away from me, really.

"Are . . . you sure you're okay?"

"Sure," I echoed.

He kissed my hand gently. I almost smacked him across the face. "I love you," he whispered.

The red-stained collar of his shirt flooded my eyes. I turned my head away.

I pretended to be asleep when Robert returned. He let me be, and the soup went cold on the night table. After a sleepless night, I slid quietly out of bed, dressed, and left for the showroom early. For a while, I was alone at my drawing table. I sketched obliviously, the questions rising in my mind like a river in a storm: Who was she? The wife of a client? Could it have been an innocent accident? What did she have that I didn't? How long had he been seeing her? Did he love her? I mean, *love* her?

All I knew at the moment was that I was not going to be one of those hysterical wives whose operatic behavior sends her man packing. At least, not yet. My instincts told me that I needed more information before I confronted him. And then, maybe, *I* would be the one packing.

When my staff arrived, I was relieved that there were no crises; it was a day without snags. Almost like a gift, I was left largely undisturbed, alone in my office. Immersed in the creation of a new men's line, I imagined and sketched, becoming increasingly obsessed with that smear of red lipstick.

Around four o'clock, my private phone line rang. Half-expecting, half-dreading the conversation I knew I was going to have, I let it ring as I tied, then untied, the bow tie around a mannequin's neck. He was otherwise dressed in my own creation: a loose-fitting, deconstructed suit. I held one end of the bow tie in each hand after I punched the speaker button on the phone.

"Hello?" I answered.

"Zoey, how you doing?"

My husband, Robert, of course.

"Fine," I said. I could hear the sounds of cranes, forklifts, engines—the sounds of construction—beyond his voice. I envisioned him sitting in the Cherokee. Why had he gone outside to call me? He wouldn't want to lie in the office, I imagined. Someone might have overheard.

"You won't believe what these fucking guys want now," he went on.

"Let me guess," I answered. "They want you to work late."

"They want to expand the damn lobby," he explained. "I'm gonna be here all night doing elevations."

"I understand," I lied. Not so hard; he was lying, too.

"Look," he said softly, "just close your eyes and think about Bali, okay? 'Cause that's where I'm taking you as soon as this is over. Okay? Sorry, angel. I love you."

If I could have ripped the bow tie into pieces, I would have. I gripped it as tightly as I could as I said, "You, too . . . Bye."

After I tossed the bow tie into the garbage can, I called my assistant. "Sally, I'm leaving for the day. If anyone calls, I'm not reachable."

I had to see it for myself.

I drove to the construction site across town. The Cherokee was still out front. I waited. Not ten minutes later, Robert emerged from his office. I needed to see his face. He hopped—yes, hopped—into the Jeep. It was essential to see his eyes.

But even more, I had to see *her*.

I followed him to Vertigo, a restaurant/club we'd been to many times. It was out of the way, discreet and progressive. After I parked, I waited a few minutes, both hands clutching the steering wheel just as I had clutched the bow tie before going in. As if I were the only one in the restaurant, I looked neither left nor right as I strode to the bar.

"What can I get for you?" the bartender asked.

I was relieved I didn't know him. "A Pinot Noir, please," I replied.

As I sipped my wine, I surveyed the room. I didn't even bother trying to hide; I was beyond caring. Robert was alone at a two-top in one of the recessed corners of the room. Connecting all four corners of the place was the dance floor, where several couples danced, unwound, seduced.

After a few minutes, a woman came in and approached Robert's table. He stood and welcomed her with a knowing kiss.

So, that was *her*. Tall, curvy, angelic. Fuck. Hair tumbling to midback. I noticed it was the same wheat color as mine. Her angelic face was so much more sculpted than my heart-shaped one; my even features would be easily forgotten in the presence of her pouty lips alone. And behind that pout, I saw something else in her expression—a restlessness, maybe a sadness? I don't even want to mention her big breasts, her black fitted skirt suit, Red Shoes, and her perfect black pumps.

He kissed her!

They approached the dance floor, dancing close and slow. Robert had dressed carefully in a casual black suit with a white T-shirt. I was mesmerized, both by seeing him move in ways I had known only in relation to myself and by the sight of her. How luscious she was as she danced with him, against him, into him. It filled me with a strange longing that I was not familiar with, that I could not identify. Did I feel left out? Excluded? Abandoned? Bereft? Such an odd assortment of sensation and emotion.

I witnessed their intimacy; they knew each other well. The realization made me want to throw up. I made my way to the bathroom, finding myself staring at my image in the mirror with a stranger's eyes.

What was this moment? What was happening? How could my life be so unbelievably different than what I'd thought it was? How could the man I had loved forever love someone else, make love to someone else? Pretend that everything was the same between us? Bring me soup after being with *her*?

I admit it: There was nothing in my life that could compare to this. For the first time ever, I felt smaller than small, vaporous, nonexistent. I was paralyzed as I stood before that mirror, suddenly comparing my features to those of the absolute beauty my Robert was obviously completely addicted to.

Fuck, I hated her. And him, I . . .

The bathroom door swung open. Red Shoes, who do you think it was, barreling in with her own needs, her own reality?

Immobile, I was still in front of the mirror. As if we were old friends, she said, "Hi," and she planted herself beside me. She glanced into the mirror and reached into her bag, removed some blush and brushed it into her cheeks.

"Hi," I echoed. *Fuck you, cunt.*

For a moment, we looked at each other in the mirror. I confess, Red Shoes, we studied each other the way women do: What are your best points? What are your worst?

As I'd noticed earlier, our wheat-colored hair was exactly the same shade. Our skin shared a certain paleness. She was a bit taller, but that might have been thanks to her pumps. My shoulders were wider, more elegant; hers slumped forward. Probably because of her enormous breasts. Mine were mere toddlers in comparison. My cheeks flushed with humiliation at this discovery. How could I hide? I could not even move.

"Quite extraordinary," she eventually said. "You have beautiful lips."

"Thanks," I muttered. What was this? Why was she talking to me at all?

"But if I were you," she went on, "I'd use a darker shade. Look, we have the same hair, the same skin tone. I think you should use mine."

As I stood speechless, she rummaged in her bag until she found her lipstick.

That lipstick. The one smeared on his collar.

She reached one hand up to my chin.

"No, really, it's fine," I blurted. "It's okay." She was *touching* me.

"Oh, don't be such a scaredy cat," she purred. "You'll look beautiful in it."

With two quick swipes, she deftly applied the lipstick to my mouth. I was stunned.

"You see?" she said. "It's as simple as that. A change of lipstick can change your whole life."

I could only stare at myself in the mirror. The lipstick's delicate aroma overwhelmed me. I flashed to the discovery of Robert's stained shirt; how the promise of spring, of everything new, which lay hidden in that scent had drawn me to it.

"Bye," she called as she left.

I said nothing.

A change of lipstick can change your whole life.

I reached for a tissue and wiped the red smear into nothingness.

Eventually, I made my way back to the bar. I sipped another glass of wine as I waited, anticipating the after-dinner scenario. Would they linger in the Jeep? Head back to her place?

After they left the restaurant, I followed Robert's Cherokee to a motel right off the highway. A seedy motel! I stayed behind, clutching the steering wheel as they entered their room, then stepped gingerly into the parking lot. They were so caught up with each other they paid no attention to the window drapes that hung awry, creating a perfect gap through which I could see most of the room from my perch on the curb. The window itself was open a few inches, which made it possible for me to hear some of what they said to each other.

Robert sat on a chair watching her. Dancing slowly, she began to undress. She moved sensually, swaying her hips as she removed the jacket of her tight black suit. Nothing but a black bra underneath. Fuck, her breasts were like small planets, straining to bust out of the flimsy material. Robert was mesmerized; I could see it in his stillness as he gazed at her.

The truth was, I couldn't take my eyes from her, either. Her legs went on forever, her hips a sexy pendulum as she inched down her skirt. It was like a dream watching her drift into one corner and turn around, balancing on her pumps. Barely covered by black lace panties, she swung her glorious ass from side to side, black garters circling her upper thighs. She turned to face him once more, prancing forward on her languidly long legs, shaking her torso so that the mountains that were her breasts shimmied, too, begging to be climbed.

Her beauty made me shudder; she seemed so untouchable. I could not stop watching her, and neither could he. She picked up a lamp and started to dance with it, removing the lampshade so that the glow of the bulb softly illuminated her body. She hypnotized us both as she trailed the lamp over her flesh, creating paths of light along her thighs, her cleavage, her crotch.

She glanced toward the window. I flinched. Did she see me?

She didn't seem to. Eventually, she put down the lamp and lifted both hands to unclasp her bra. As her breasts tumbled from it, I felt a part of myself tumble inside, too. Robert seemed pinned to his chair; I could easily make out the hard-on straining against his pants. So could she, obviously, for she sashayed forward then and slowly knelt between his legs.

It was an indescribable experience to watch my husband finally touch her. He traced his fingers tenderly through her wild mane, barely meeting the edges of her face. He mapped her shoulders, hovering delicately at the curve of her neck. Eventually, he lowered both hands to her naked breasts. He cupped the weight of each blooming mound in his palm, and even with fingers uncurled completely to grasp each one, they were just too big to contain.

His eyes brightened like those of a child, presented with not one but two enormous, delectable treats. As she stretched her fingers across the top of his thighs, he began to massage each breast softly. He pressed the fleshy moons together and slowly tantalized the sudden hollow created between them with the supple underside of his thumb. Finally letting them loose, she sighed as he squeezed a handful of each before focusing on her areolas. They were a much darker color than mine, a cross between freshly turned earth and lollipop red. As he began to circle their outside edges with his fingertips, I knew it would be but a moment before her nipples hardened and she closed her eyes. She arched back then, her hands gripping his thighs to keep her balance, her pleasure spiraling as her beloved babies poked out even more, nearly filling the space between them.

Every man's dream, right, Red Shoes? To have a woman kneeling between your legs, pushing her rack at you like that, begging for more? It was certainly a dream of *his*—the stiff cock straining against his crotch the proof. I heard the familiar groan rise in his throat, the one that would climb from his chest when his lust teemed. I confess: It was like it was rising in *me*, too.

Was this what it was like to watch erotica? At one moment, perhaps, you felt what one of the lovers would feel, and the next, you'd feel what the other one felt. Except in my case, of course, there was an emotional element the innocent viewer would never have to grapple with. I mean, I was *married* to him, after all. I was actually witnessing *infidelity*. Even so—or maybe exactly because of that fact—there was a part of me that didn't want to miss a moment, a gesture, between them.

He leaned forward, one hand sliding to the nape of her neck. As his mouth met hers, they both sighed. He still held one breast in his hand as his tongue played hers, his fingertips finally finding her waiting nipple. I watched as he held her lips between his own and rolled her hard nub between two fingers. He was waiting for the moan that would escape her then, that he would take into his mouth and echo back with the sound of a lover knowingly stirring desire.

Which I felt in the back of my throat.

As their sounds and breaths mingled, they began to kiss more deeply. When his hand returned to her other breast and played its virgin nipple, a slight, trilling sound rose from her. She seemed less fragile than purely innocent then, though it seemed hard to believe a beauty such as she had not had many lovers already.

When she reached between his legs, he brushed her hand away.

That was a surprise.

But then I understood: Mr. Control.

Still on her knees, he continued to tweak her nipples. Their color deepened. Like mine, her breasts were obviously very sensitive; she shivered beneath his touch, her hands gripping his thighs tighter. He smiled as his fingers climbed over her ample mounds, clasping each one before pressing them together. She moaned as he squeezed and then abandoned them: *Squeeze, release. Squeeze, relinquish.*

She squirmed each time he let them go, allowing them to hang naked in the air. After a few seconds, he would touch them again.

My feelings were mixed. Even though a part of me was deeply

appalled at the adulterous scene before me, I also felt the pungent tingle of desire inch along my spine to my cunt.

He leaned forward and cupped each handful, suddenly pulling her close as he did. She caught her breath as he firmly gripped each fleshy globe and then started to slap them together. Mine were too small to do that, but they stung now anyway. When a car pulled into the parking lot, I strode quickly toward mine, slipping back quietly once whoever it was had gone into his room. My nipples were hard against my blouse; it took effort not to touch them.

Perched outside the window again, I saw her breathing quicken as he intensified his movements, both hands on her breasts. He watched her quivering flesh jiggle and sway, the flush of excitement crawling up her neck as he massaged each handful and then clapped her babies together. At a certain point, he bent his forearm so that her mounds lay upon it. That freed his other hand to punish her nipples, twisting them slowly between his thumb and forefinger. I would cream instantly when he teased me like that. He would tug the tip of each one, squeeze it, and then flick his tongue across it.

With each gesture, a delighted gasp escaped her: "Oh! Ah! Ohhh!"

"Bend over," he suddenly ordered.

But she only looked at him.

"I want to see them dance," he said. "On your hands and knees, now."

But she only laughed.

He smiled. "Good girls do what they're told. Bad girls get spanked."

Before she could react, he leaned forward and swept her panties down to her thighs. Then he grabbed her by the hips and dragged her across his lap. In one smooth move, he yanked her panties down her legs and over her ankles. He parted her legs with a firm knee, and followed that surprise with a resounding *slap* across both of her buttocks.

Red Shoes, her rack was dancing now. Fuck. And mine was begging for it.

Her breasts dangled in midair, in full view of me, her legs spread in a "V." The puddle of desire that was her pussy seemed to be directly in front of my mouth, daring me to drink it in. Her breasts began to bob with each *smack* he meted out. She squirmed as he spanked her, giving a startled yelp with each slap as he paddled the tender flesh with a steady, relentless hand. Increasingly frantic, her legs scissored the air.

As she struggled to escape the pelting, he eventually dipped two fingers into her wet, wanting cave, spreading her labia with his other hand so he could watch how she squeezed him, tried to hold him inside. He'd pump her a few times and then pull out, leaving her open and empty. She writhed for more, her legs flailing.

I have to admit, it thrilled me. Every plunge, every kick.

Fuck. In the midst of the biggest betrayal I'd ever experienced, I was turned on—utterly, unbelievably, *enormously.*

He kept the lips of her snatch parted and slowly spanked her clitoris, sliding the same punishing fingers to the entrance of her glistening hole. He teased her there before sliding the fingers back to her swollen pearl, caressing her until she trembled. I imagined how the flesh of her ass tingled when it began to shiver, her legs quaking as she approached climax.

But he wouldn't let her come. Instead, he started over as she whimpered, returning to her now quivering, pink buttocks with his open hand. He rubbed the flesh gently at first, kneading the soft handfuls before massaging both buttocks with his palm. He held her legs down this time, slipping one of his over both her ankles. Then he started to spank—and fuck—her all over again.

I was mesmerized, my slit a river of desire.

When she finally began to cry, he let a long line of saliva drip from his lips to her anus. She squirmed, her ass lifting in response.

I felt my own buttocks clench as I imagined the moist heat of his spit landing on that ultra-sensitive spot. I had no doubt that his dick was ready to spill, too.

He sucked his thumb, making her wait. Then he slid it inside her asshole, which made her arch back with a cry. He left off spanking then, and focused on her dripping gash. He plowed two soaked fingers into her, then pulled out and drummed her clit while his thumb slowly plugged her ass. She bucked with each thrust, her legs still bound by his.

It was irresistible how the trembling finally overtook her, her ass lifting to receive each plunge, her climax rippling through her like a rising wave buffeted by wind. Each convulsion twisted through her, every part of her surrendering to his insistence.

That would delight him, I knew. He would coo sweet nothings to her now, wait for her body to absorb the hot, streaming pleasure completely. Then he would fuck her exactly the same way once more, yet this time, twice as fast.

Only after that would he lay her down on the bed and mount her, his untouched rod throbbing so much he'd nearly come each time he thrust inside her.

But not Mr. Control.

He'd make it last.

Hey Red Shoes, who do you think taught him how to make love like that? The easiest way to make a woman want to do what you want is to make her come before you ride her.

And how she had come? She lay limp across his lap, twitching all the way to her fingers and toes as he withdrew his thumb slowly from her anus, let his fingers linger tenderly on her clit. He waited for her breathing to slow down, for her gasping sounds to still. As she turned onto her side, he slid his arms around her, one under her ribs, the other around her waist.

As she panted, he began to rock her slowly.

What a sweet moment.

I'd seen enough. The reality was, I could barely make it to my car. My body felt weak and yet enormously electrified. The idea of going home to our bed seemed a confused, strangely sickening world away. I drove aimlessly for a while, ending up back at the showroom. I tried not to feel what I felt; I tried to sketch. I found myself pretending that one hand was not between my legs while the other revealed shadowy figures on my drawing pad.

My bud was as swollen as it would have been had Robert already sucked it and made me come. My snatch felt empty and wanting, needing to fuck. How could this be when I had just witnessed my own husband's disloyalty with *her*?

Images of her breasts and how he had punished them until she writhed filled my mind. How she yelped as he slapped her ass cheeks leapt through my entire being. Two of my fingers pumped my snatch as my other hand spread my lips and spanked my own clit. It seemed mere seconds before my orgasm clapped through me as if with a thousand tiny, ecstatic hands.

He had fucked me forever, of course. But how come he had never spanked me like that? Was I not a bad girl? Was I unspankable?

. . .

I thought about what I had seen for days. Told Robert I was on a work deadline. Stayed out of the house as much as I could. Avoided making love, which was easy, as Robert had come down with a bad cold.

And then one night, I'd had enough of myself.

Every day, every morning, in every fantasy, all I thought about was *her*. I looked down at the sketches on my drawing table. More than anything, they looked like me. Well, me if I were a man, since I had apparently sketched myself decked out in my new line's main event: a hip, tight, glove of a suit. It was a kind of genderless creation that had risen from an unfamiliar place inside me, I realized.

I mean, why did this woman turn me on so much?

When I replayed the night between them in my mind, it was *me* who was *him* touching her, yet that perspective would instantly somersault, and I would become *me* being touched by *him* as if I were *her*. What was more confusing was that because I knew him so completely I was familiar with everything he felt, too. So I was everyone at once, which made me man and woman, lover and beloved, consumed and longing.

And always so trusting, always so loyal. The good girl, that'd always been me. Exactly where had that gotten me? A life that was a lie? Fuck, yes. A spanking like she'd gotten? Fuck, no!

I walked over to a mannequin and removed his necktie. I rummaged through my samples to find trousers and a suit jacket small enough to fit me. After I stripped, I wrapped a sheer silk scarf around my breasts. Then I proceeded to dress myself in a sharply starched dress shirt, the tie knotted around my neck longer than any cock I'd ever seen. I left on my white lace panties—the untainted world of my femininity beneath my disguise—and pulled on a pair of pleated trousers.

And where was I going, Red Shoes?

You guessed it: Vertigo. How did I know she would be there? I didn't, only that I had to see her. Robert was home, still sick. I called him and lied: "Honey, it's me. Something just came up. They want me to speak on some panel tonight. I know it sucks, but just close your eyes and think of Bali. . . . Love you."

He accepted that, of course. A numb heart made it easy to lie. After I hung up the phone, I finished off my outfit with a few threads of a moustache and something every gentleman needs: a fedora. How else might you tip your hat to a lady? And how else would I hide my hair?

As I drove to the club I had to talk myself down, force my mind to stop questioning my motives, and convince myself to go with the moment. I had sketched it, after all.

When I walked in, there she was. Elegant in a tight black dress and shawl, she danced with a dark, handsome dude in black sunglasses.

Red Shoes, it was my turn.

Aping Robert's casual, cocky stride, I walked to the bar. I downed the whiskey I ordered in one gulp and noticed a woman seated alone near me. She was probably no older than me, her curly hair hiding her face, her nervous fingers playing with her wine glass.

Life wasn't always easy for a single woman. It took guts to plant yourself in the middle of a club and hope for action.

After two deep breaths, willing my voice to deepen as well, I asked her to dance.

There were several other couples on the dance floor, but I was able to see *her* every move. After a few dances, I thanked my partner and then sidled up to her, cutting in. I took her arm and drew her into both of mine, and she did not resist. We started to sway to the music and as I held her close, I breathed in her captivating scent, the perfume of her lipstick. Cut now with the heat of her perspiration, she was beyond ripe.

My senses filled; she was intoxicating. Her breasts were like magnets. Now I knew what it felt like to be *him*.

My hands started roaming over her body. I couldn't help it; there was no resisting her. She capitulated, tugging me closer, resting her head on my shoulder. Abruptly, she lifted her mane and dug into my eyes with her own.

"I saw you staring at me," she whispered.

I said nothing. What could I say?

"Do you like what you see?" she went on.

"I do," I whispered back.

She smiled. "The owner's a friend of mine. Would you like to see his office?"

I stopped dancing. She squeezed my hand and led me away from the dance floor.

The office was wood paneled, cozy with an oversized leather couch and chairs. Pictures of women were everywhere—in frames on the walls, piled atop the tables, loose black and whites scattered across the desk. Some were naked, some barely dressed, a handful in hats smiling directly into the camera, others suggestively turned away.

What was this, a fuck pad?

She had taken my arm and led me here, only now letting me go as she closed the door behind us. I turned to face her. She looked at me in a way I did not recognize—asking, daring? Mentally, I flashed to her kneeling on the floor between *his* legs, her breasts jutting toward him. Her whole chest had heaved, begging him with each breath to bully those babies into abandon.

Act like a man in control, I exhorted myself.

"Take off the shawl," I ordered.

That look again—imploring, yet challenging. She slid the black fabric slowly over her body, letting it eventually fall to the floor.

"Lisa," she whispered. "I'm Lisa."

"Take off the dress, Lisa," I responded.

Without another word, she did. Defiant in black stockings, black panties, and high heels only, she stood before me. I could not stop my eyes from sweeping over her phenomenal curves, her gargantuan breasts. Fuck, were they *real*?

"Now you," she said.

"When I'm ready," I answered.

She moved toward me, barely an inch away.

"I think you're ready," she said, breathing heavily.

She started to caress me, tried to kiss me with her red painted lips. I moved back, pushing myself against a wall, just as I had in my own bathroom. Lisa was right there next to me, one hand pulling lightly on my necktie, the other softly tracing the outline of my face.

Again, I pulled away. That was when she reached forward and yanked off my hat. My hair tumbled down.

Exposed!

Stunned, I could not move.

"You're his wife, aren't you?" she whispered.

What? She knew it was me? Tonight? At the motel? At the club, the first time? My mind raced. She started to stroke my hair. I said nothing. Tenderly, she ran a few fingers over the silly moustache above my lip and slowly teased it off between her buttery fingertips.

"Those lips . . . so beautiful . . . so fucking beautiful . . ." she said with a gasp.

She had told me that in the club bathroom that night. Well, it was my turn to say something now.

"I was outside the motel room window," I blurted. "I watched you make love to my husband."

"I know," she said quietly.

So she *had* seen me. She still stroked my hair; strangely, I allowed her to.

"The question is," she went on, "which one of us were you watching? Him or me?"

There was no other word for it: I swooned.

"Did . . . did he see me, too?" I finally managed.

"No," she said. She began to touch me, my shoulders, nape, jaw. "It's our little secret. You're so fucking beautiful," she said, practically purring.

She kissed my neck slowly, her tongue lingering at the curve of my shoulder. Her lips were like wet silk, so plump and perfect. Each unexpected kiss streamed through me.

"Are you frightened?" she whispered.

I could only nod. My gaze was riveted on her naked breasts, each breath lifting them toward me.

"Of change?" she continued. One hand still held my tie. She began to loosen it. That was good.

On the wall across from us, I noticed a picture of two women. Like a jury, they seemed to be staring directly at me.

"Of a new lipstick?" she questioned. "Ah, don't move."

She found her bag on the floor and took out her lipstick. I watched as she sauntered over to me again, my knees nearly buckling at her beauty. Feelings collided inside me—confusion, dread, desire.

"It's called Rampant Red," she explained.

I didn't—couldn't—move.

She smiled as she twisted the lipstick open, lifting it to my mouth.

"Red lipstick on a woman is a dangerous thing," she cooed as she painted it on my lips. "And *you* are a dangerous woman. Come, tell me what you're really afraid of?"

Her lipstick. That scent. Those breasts.

"Of losing your husband?" she pressed.

Our eyes locked.

Lisa whispered, "I'm scared, too."

I grabbed her then, around the waist.

"No, you're not," I stated.

She touched my chin lightly.

"Yes, I am. Your husband . . . I needed him. . . . Like I need you now. . . ." she admitted.

She needed me? Her fingertips trailed behind my ears. My hands seemed to float up her waist.

Inadvertently, my gaze took in a photo on the wall of a woman's face hidden by a feather mask. As I focused on it, I wanted to hide. What had I imagined, that I would show up disguised as a guy and hope that she would find me irresistible? That it would somehow prove that she wasn't in love with Robert? *Was* she in love with my husband? Then what was she doing here, dancing with some other guy? And now, look at us, fondling each other—woman to woman.

"Are you in love with my husband?" I blurted out. My hands fell from the warmth of her waist.

She smiled, her palms resting on my shoulders. "*In* love, no. I just loved making love with him," she replied.

"Why?" I pressed. "There are other men, unmarried men . . ."

"He's good at it," she interrupted. "If a guy's been married for a long time, he's one of two things. He's bad at sex because his wife won't screw him or he's good at sex because she taught him everything he knows."

She leaned closer, her handfuls swaying hypnotically. "My guess is the latter in your case."

I swallowed hard. What was happening? This close, her breath felt like a sultry wind. It fluttered against the hidden walls of my pussy. How do you go from being strangers to being lovers, Red Shoes? How do you step from separation into passion? Reach out and begin to touch another, invite them into your energy, your being, your life?

"I don't want to take your husband away from you. I just want to feel. I can't feel on my own anymore. . . ." she continued.

Lisa reached for my hands. She teased them slowly toward her rack.

"Make me feel," she said, with a heavy breath.

I resisted. What did she mean, she couldn't feel? She released my hands and unbuttoned the top buttons of my shirt. The world went into slow motion as she pulled back the fabric and began to kiss my bare shoulders.

"Please," Lisa pleaded, "make me feel. Can you make me feel?"

Her lips on my shoulders shivered through me. She thrust her breasts against mine—such sweet pillows! Oh, they were real all right, literally pulsing with the heat of desire. Instinctively, I found myself yielding to the melting sensation within that they caused. My hands found her waist again and pulled her closer.

She moaned.

Without a doubt, I could make her feel.

"There you are," she cooed. She unbuttoned my shirt slowly, pulled it to my waist. My babies were bound only by a sheer silk scarf.

"You're so beautiful . . . so brave . . ." she whispered.

Barely making contact, her fingertips approached my breasts. I shuddered.

Lisa said, "That's it, my beauty. Feel me."

Her fingers grazed my nipples as if she were touching her own, it seemed. Telling them to remember how much they liked to be approached, in precisely this way.

Do it slowly, as if you're waking up to it. Your soft fingertips almost meeting your moons of flesh, but as if with a new awareness. Tentative, hesitant, respectful, intrigued. It was without a thought that my nipples jumped to attention as she touched them, the slight, sheer protection over them but a ripple from gloriously naked sensation.

What was it like to have an unintended lover caress your flesh? Without knowing it, I seemed to recognize her tender touch. I reached up and untied my flimsy, makeshift bra, my rack now entirely exposed as the tidbit of material wafted to the floor. We both sighed as her fingers landed on my achingly sensitive areolas.

She watched me as she made small circles around the tender pink flesh, gauging my response. At first, her fingers were feathery. Did I like it like that? Or harder? Faster?

The truth was, I liked it all. I leaned closer, one hand reaching around her nape to pull her toward me, to breathe in her scent. I wondered what kissing her would be like.

Kissing her?

Here I was, a married woman, fantasizing about kissing another woman. And not only another women, *the* other woman.

Too much, too soon. I released her, my hands falling again to her waist, and then slowly creeping up her sides to her breasts. We looked into each other's eyes as my fingers began to mirror exactly how hers touched mine. When I circled her areolas, she sighed. When I pinched her hard nubs between two fingers, she moaned. When my fingers spread to clasp the weight of each breast in my hand, she trembled.

And when we encircled each other with our arms and our breasts crushed together, we gasped.

We pulled apart, Lisa's eyes bright. Barely moving, we began to brush our nipples against each other's and made sweet, amazed sounds as arrows of scintillating bliss arced through us.

As the sensations deepened, my slit flooded and I felt myself dissolve into her arms. More than anything, I wanted to kiss her. All choice was gone. I absolutely had to.

"Come here," I whispered.

Imagine a swatch of swollen, heated velvet. Those were her lips. Imagine a sleek, resilient sail as the wind lifts it. That was her tongue.

How luscious was this moment, melting through me, inside me, melting *me*. I could barely stand, losing my balance as the kiss deepened. Lisa responded by wrapping me completely in her arms. We swayed as we kissed, a torrent of desire rushing through every synapse as our tongues found each other's, our breasts pressed together, our bellies soft as butter.

At this point, my entire *being* felt like butter—slippery, supple, ready to be spread all over the place!

It felt like our first kiss might never have ended, Lisa's fingers climbing to the nape of my neck, pulling me even closer as her tongue fucked my mouth like a little cock. With each thrust, my legs felt even weaker. Our breasts still crushed together, Lisa's hands trickled down over my shoulders until her arms wound around me again, slowly backing me toward the couch.

We fell in a heap onto the soft pillows. The couch was wide enough so that the two of us could easily have lain side by side, yet Lisa was above me on her knees, straddling me. Naked except for her black stockings, black panties, and high heels, she arched back and inched off her pumps. Her breasts were at eye level now, and I felt like a pubescent boy as I ogled them, masterpieces that they were. She could obviously see what an impact they had, for she leaned forward, making them sway from side to side with a slight shimmy of her torso.

"I'm hungry for your mouth," she whispered. "Are you hungry for my titties?"

Hungry? More than hunger ached at the bottom of my throat. She inched forward until one nipple stood erect a mere moment from my mouth. As she gripped the back of the couch with both hands, I wrapped mine around her breast and approached it slowly with my lips. I drank in the earthy umber hue of her areola with my eyes before the tip of my tongue finally met her nipple. It was the diameter of my little finger, and seemingly, just as firm.

Imagine doing something for the first time, Red Shoes. How it feels to be in the midst of discovery itself, completely captivated by the moment. There was a childlike element to it, an innocence. Smitten by all of it, lust sprawled across my every nerve ending.

Who was this miraculous creature?

The tip of my tongue lingered before I began to lap her nipple. I circled it. I wrapped my lips around it. My tongue thrummed against her moist little mountain, and like a song, Lisa made sounds of pleasure I had only heard myself make. How that echoed through me, making the deep inner tissue of my gash tremble.

She moaned as I pressed her tender nub between my lips. I nibbled it. I licked it. I kissed it.

"Suck it," she suddenly said.

The invitation was as irresistible as she was. Like a desert seeking water, an ocean billowing toward shore, a mountain needing sky, that was my mouth on her breast. With both hands, I pushed her mounds together, my tongue sailing from one to the other. What a glorious world it was; I had become a wanton explorer of this beguiling new terrain.

And I hadn't even ventured to the cosmos between her legs.

Did she sense my curiosity? Or did she just naturally want to satisfy her own as she lifted herself away from my mouth and suddenly slid her body down my torso? She knelt on the floor as she unfastened the button at the waist of my pants. I tried to sit up, my mouth suddenly bereft, but she pushed me back.

"Oh no, baby. It's my turn," she cooed. "You've been sucking me, and I can't wait any longer. I need to taste you."

With a sigh, I lay back. I looked into her eyes as she pulled my pants down and discovered the tip of my white panties. We both giggled at the contrast. After she pulled the trousers over my ankles, she trickled her fingers up my calves to my thighs, where she traced slight circles and began to kiss the delicate flesh behind my knees and along my inner thighs. Her fingers felt like warm water, and her tongue like a hot little beast. She flattened it as she licked my soft flesh, she hardened it like a tiny sex warrior as she explored new territory, she drove it like a race driver along the tender tissue of the road that was me.

As her hands reached the place where the edge of my thighs met my pelvis, I shuddered. I felt her breath against the crotch of my pure little panties, and her thumbs inched like velvet under its edges. She slid one thumb into the puddle that was deepening there, and the other onto my hot clit.

Neither of us moved then, except for her damp hot breath that teased like a sexy wind. My moans rose up and out of my throat, giving voice to my intensifying excitement.

Still she did not move. What was she waiting for? I felt the pulse of my desire surface in the exact places where she touched me, and she let out a slow sigh. Ah, so that was what she was waiting for. The pulsing quickened as she pulled her thumb away and closed her lips around my clitoris. Her breath was like a torch against my panties. She licked the already sodden fabric, which sent a searing bolt of bliss throughout my entire body.

I could not stand it; I slid my hands to hers. "Take them off!" I cried.

"Good girls say *please*," she murmured.

"Please!" I begged.

She hooked her forefingers under the waistline and dragged my panties slowly down my legs, over my ankles. As I watched her, she spread my legs, leaning forward so that they could lay over her shoulders as she approached my gash with her mouth.

"Are you ready for me, beautiful?" she whispered. Her breath against my bare cunt challenged everything I knew that was *me*, I wanted it so much.

"Please," I whispered, "please . . ."

She licked her luscious lips before she pushed her tongue into the aching river I had become. I gasped. She dove straight in, no hesitation. It was exactly what I wanted.

I tried to stay still as she fucked me with her tongue once, twice, again. I lost count as her thumb went back to my bud and daubed it lightly. I began to understand a woman's touch in a way I had never known; she responded to *me* responding to *her*. So when I shimmied my hips, her tongue licked me faster. When my hips slowed down, her fingers fucked me more slowly.

My hands reached down, grabbing her hair as her lips closed around my clit and she started to suck me. I felt the inner walls of my snatch grab at the mirage of her fingers inside me. My heels pressed against her bare back, pulling her closer.

"Fuck me!" I cried.

She moaned as my ass shook beneath her mouth. I felt the sound race through me, my own pulsing desire reaching out to her.

"Please," I panted, "please fuck me."

Her tongue lapped at my clitoris. Again, without hesitation, she plowed two fingers inside me. All of me, my hips, my pussy, my sweet ass, rose up to meet her, wanting her to go deeper, to fill me with *her*—the wild, daring animal that she was.

"More!" I cried.

Again, she wasted no time. She pushed a third finger in, and then she waited once more, motionless. I writhed from the rushing sensation. As she continued to flick her tongue over my hard pearl, she started to pump me. Obviously, I did not know what it was like to be fucked by a woman. I did not expect that her fingers, a part of her hand, a part of her arm, a part of her shoulder, would suddenly feel like a massive cock, fucking me with that much intensity. Oh, it was different from Robert, whose rod I recognized as if it were part of my own body; I had been with him that long, loved him that much. With her cock-arm fucking me this way, though, she felt so much bigger than my husband ever had!

She pulled out to the tips of her fingers, ringed her tongue around my clit at least a dozen times, and then waited again. I almost burst into tears from the frustration.

"Please!" I cried. "Don't stop!"

My hands were still in her hair. I pulled on it and she lifted her head to look at me.

"Do you like it?" she said.

"Yes," I said as I panted.

"How much?" she teased.

How could I answer that? I shook my hips, wriggling toward her. My slash was literally dripping.

"Do you want more?" she cooed.

"Pleeeease. . . . " I begged.

"What do you want—my tongue or my fingers?"

"Both!" I blurted.

"My pleasure," she said with a purr. She plowed her fingers back inside as she lowered her tongue onto my fat pearl once again.

It was like a dance then, as my hips rose to meet her touch. Like a dream, as she slammed into me with her cock-arm while her tongue flicked across my clit. Another world as she swirled that superb mouth around my ocean.

And it was in this world, where nothing else existed but this moment, these delicious sensations, my overflowing cunt, when something changed. Changed in the way lightning infiltrates the sky, suddenly and with so much force.

I sensed that the dance, the moment, the world, was not enough. Instead, a deeper part of me was after what the dance was danced for, or maybe, the dance *behind* the dance.

I sat up suddenly, causing the angle of her fingers to change and accidentally pound my cervix. It hurt and felt good at the same time.

"Why do you want to fuck me?" I asked.

Her face. So much expression. Now, it registered surprise.

"I . . . I want to please you," she explained.

"Why?"

"Because life can be hard. This can be easy," she said.

She curled her fingers inside me and I gasped. It was like I had an itch deep inside and she knew exactly where to scratch.

"Am I close?" she whispered.

I leaned forward and kissed her on the mouth. It was slick with my juice and she tasted like me, buttery and smooth. It was another sweet surprise.

"That's right, baby," she said, breathing heavily. "Give me your tongue."

And I did.

The instant I slid my tender little tool into her mouth, she closed her lips around it. She slowly slid her fingers out of me and reached up with both hands to hold my head as she began to suck my tongue. If I wasn't already sitting I might have fallen down. I groaned as she pulled back so that her lips held only its tip, but just as suddenly her lips circled it again and took it deep into her mouth. Fuck if she wasn't giving my tongue a blow job!

At that moment, my tongue felt like my clit and I thought I would burst, topple over. Her breasts began to bob as she rocked back and forth, and I reached out, grabbing them, anchoring me, making her moan.

I gripped her nipples as she blew my tongue. I wanted to grind my snatch against her so I could come right then, my bud ached so badly.

Again, as if reading my mind, she pulled her lips completely away and grazed my breasts with hers. A sweet agony pulsed through me.

"And I want you to feel so much pleasure you will have nowhere to go but to explode," she said. "Is that enough for you?"

My gaze was riveted on her beautiful face. I could only nod as I wrapped my arms around her neck and pulled her close. I wanted her breath, her eyelashes, her lips, her rack. I wanted them all over my body, all at once.

"Fuck me with your tongue," I pleaded. "Let me feel you inside me."

She pushed me back down with a smile. My slit was an ocean and she was its explorer, her fingers diving back in, her tongue sailing across my blooming clit. She licked me once, she pumped me once. She licked me twice, she plugged me twice. She wrapped her lips around my throbbing bud and sucked gently, once, again, more. I writhed beneath her and she held me down with her other hand, reaching up my torso and landing on one of my breasts. As she took my nipple between two fingers, the fiery feeling charged down my spine, up through my buttocks, and then surfaced on my clitoris. One more flick of her tongue and the walls of my pussy fluttered against her fingers as the climax fired through me with a million licks of flame.

Red, do you think my sizzling heat scorched her tongue? Oh no, she merely lightened the pressure, each precise lick searing every synapse of my being as I bucked and burst, again, and again. Unbelievably, again.

Finally, I collapsed and she fell against me, both of us gasping for air. I pulled her up on top of me, and we lay like that until our breathing quieted. Then I curled my body around hers and rolled her onto her back.

Her turn.

. . .

When I arrived home, it was late. I tossed my hat onto a chair as
I entered the bedroom. Robert was asleep. I undressed quietly,
leaving nothing on but the shirt.

"Hey . . . " he said as he woke up.

I covered his lips with my finger and ran my hand tenderly
over his face. I kissed him slowly. He kissed me back. I unbuttoned the shirt, nearly naked except for the handful of fabric hidden in my fist.

What's your guess, Red Shoes? The tie? Try her panties, which
I unfolded and draped across Robert's face after I told him to close
his eyes. For a moment, he froze. As he pulled them away, he
opened his eyes and stared at me as I stood by the side of the bed.

Yes, we shared a secret. Yet it was a secret no longer. Because
now, we shared *her*.

"You . . . know her?" he managed to sputter out.

I climbed onto the bed then, straddling him. "I know everything," I said. "About her. *Her*. What she smells like. What she
tastes like. How she kisses. How she likes to fuck."

"I can't believe . . . I mean . . ."

"Relax," I said. "I understand. *Make me feel*, she says. *Can you
make me feel?* It's pretty wild, what a turn-on that line is. Then
there are her BREASTS, but you know all about them."

My ass rested directly on top of his sleepy dick. At the mention
of her rack, there was sudden interest underneath the blanket.
Who could blame him? Just remembering their weight, her nipples beneath my tongue, made my mouth water. The feeling began to flood through me, juicing my slit all over again.

He squirmed, embarrassed by his obvious excitement. I
ground against him on purpose, teasing him. I lifted my hands to

my naked breasts and petted them softly, letting him know without words that I felt titillated, too.

"So . . . so you're not mad?" he finally managed. He reached up and placed a tentative hand on my belly.

As it did when I had seen them together, a conflicting surge of emotions raced through me. I had been the outsider then; now I knew what it was to be with her. If only by omission, he had lied to me, and I had lied to him. Yet I also felt that though we had betrayed each other, because we'd been with the same woman, we shared something.

"Honey, I just fucked her!" I finally blurted.

"You . . . fucked . . . her . . ." he repeated, blinking suddenly as if trying to comprehend the meaning of the words. "You had sex with her?" His eyes widened. "I . . . didn't know you liked women."

I laughed. Mr. Confused. The baffled expression on his face made him look so young, even innocent. His cock was growing beneath my sweet ass, and I squeezed my knees against the supple poles that were his hips.

"Believe me, it was a surprise to me, too," I answered. "What I want to know is, what about you? How long have you been seeing her?"

"I'm not *seeing* her, Zoey. I mean, I was . . . *with* her twice."

I leaned forward and grabbed his hair, tugging it. "Yeah, that's what she said, too. But why should I believe you? I mean, for one thing, you broke our marriage vows."

He grabbed my hips, pulling me closer as tears sprang to his eyes. "It's you I love. I didn't mean to, never have before. But she was begging for it."

If I hadn't just been with her myself, I probably would not have believed him. But because I had, and because she *had* begged for it, I did not question him.

Instead, I ground my ass against him. I felt him all the way to his balls. He arched up to meet me.

My Robert. Nothing like that feeling anywhere else.

"Did she tell you that she needed you?" I asked.

"Angel. It's nowhere near how much I need you."

"Except you fucked her *twice*. Does that mean you need more than just me? Don't give me the cliché, 'It didn't mean a thing,' line."

"Listen, I married *you*. I'm in love with *you*. She was like—a moment. You're my whole life."

"Does that mean you're not gonna fuck her again?"

He stared at me with a look of surprise and confusion. "Well, what about *you*?"

I laughed, not really knowing the answer. Then I leaned down and began to kiss him. Red Shoes, I admit it was strange at first, having just kissed a woman's lips. The enticing aroma of her lipstick had wafted in with each breath, the taste of her lips made even more luscious by the wonder of the Rampant Red painted upon both hers and mine. His lips bore only the subtle scent of himself, his skin emanating an earthy swirl of potent virility.

My lips grazed his gently, our tongues coming together like small, fleshy oars. Our tongues entwined, expertly stroking each other's as we pushed deeper into the mysterious depths of ourselves.

"I'm sorry," he whispered.

"I'm not," I answered.

"I love you," he said.

"I love you back," I bandied.

He stabbed me with his tongue and I took it as far into my throat as I could. I would have swallowed him if I could.

My breasts dangled above his chest. He reached up and began to touch them. My nipples instantly became erect. Though Lisa had licked and sucked them superbly, they were obviously ready for my man. As he pressed my nips between his fingers, I squirmed above him. Our kisses deepened.

"I need you to fuck me." I breathed heavily.

"When?" he whispered.

"Now," I answered, pressing myself against his growing bulge.

"Let's wait," he said. "I want you dripping wet."

I smiled as I reached between my legs and then lifted a gleaming finger. I slathered his lips with my pussy sap. He responded with a sudden thrust upward. I rose to my knees, pulled the blanket aside, and lowered myself onto his stiff cock.

I needed that, his ripe dick inside me. Both of his hands cupped the cheeks of my ass, my palms resting on his chest. We stayed like that for a few minutes, feeling each other, breathing each other in, returning to our love. It was me who moved first, needing the sensation of us in action, together, connected. He responded by pulling me down, pressing into me, plunging deeper into my pussy.

I arched back, sat on his sexy cylinder and fucked him slowly. I yanked a handful of his hair a few times, whispering "Lisa." He responded by tugging my nipples and fucking me harder, asking "Did she fuck you like this?"

It was mesmerizing, how the passion and anger mingled, fueling our reconciliation. I lifted myself then, and crouched on my heels as I leaned back so that I could gain gravity and momentum. My beloved, gripping my forearms to help me balance as I rode him faster, arched against me as I sank to receive each stroke.

The room had filled with our sounds and smells. Already ripe from my time with Lisa, my desire seeped like a sharp, pungent nectar. Robert's musky juices met that scent so that the air was thick with us, our moans entering the space like musical chords.

When I lost my breath, he pulled me down onto my side, still inside my snatch. We lay entwined and unmoving again, rocking back and forth while the pleasure spiraled and spread.

"So what did you two do together?" he asked.

"Oh . . . the usual stuff," I answered.

"But neither one of you has got *this* stuff," he teased, stabbing his rod inside me.

"We didn't need it," I sparred.

"Is that right? You needed each other's cunts instead?"

"Well . . . more like we *wanted* them. You're the one who always says, 'There's nothing like tits and pussy.' I gotta say, I'm with you there."

His eyes were wide. "You mean you ate each other out?"

"I mean there's nothing like tits *and* pussy."

"Fuck! You sound like such a slut," he blurted.

"Is that bad? Maybe I am," I countered.

Our breath came quicker now. How much did we mean what we said? How much did it mean what we had done?

He suddenly pinned me on my back, lifting my legs high in the air. He grabbed my ankles and spread me wide. It was his turn now to kneel and pump me. I teased his nipples with one hand and touched myself with the other. He grunted his approval as I played with my clit, meeting each of his thrusts in my wet, welcoming hole. I gripped him inside the closer my orgasm came, slowing his pace so that I could feel every rush whirling through me.

"Did she fuck you like this?" he asked.

"Did you fuck *her* like this?" I responded.

We growled and grunted at each other, fury and nerves entwined.

Moments before he climaxed, Robert's feet fanned out, like a dancer's in first position. My love for him soared through me.

After he rammed into me once more, he clenched his ass cheeks and rocked us back and forth gently. I ground against him, my cunt about to explode, my arms around his neck. He gripped my ass harder. The instant before he came he stiffened completely, and his hot milk spurted into me as his toes twitched. My pussy walls pulsing, my cum met his as we panted and writhed together.

After about a minute, he flipped me over onto my belly. Both of us had barely caught our breath. His full weight was upon me; we were part of each other.

"You know what I'm gonna do now," he whispered.

"I need to hear you say it."

"Angel." He licked my ear. "I'm gonna fuck you in the ass, and you're gonna love it. You're gonna give yourself to me totally, inch by inch, and when we're done you're gonna already know that you want it again, need it again, more than anything else in the whole fucking world."

I could only moan.

"But first," he went on, "I'm gonna rim you with my tongue. I'm gonna lick your ass until it opens up for me and begs me for my cock."

He slid to his side, pressed against mine, and held me down with one hand on my buttocks. He rubbed my cheeks tenderly, kneading each one as if it was the most beloved handful he'd ever touched.

He slapped me lightly—once, twice, again. It was reflex, not pain, that made me flinch. Would he spank me now as he had *her*? Did I want him to? Given how much heat was happening between us at this moment, that would not be nearly enough.

"Be my good girl and get on your knees," he cooed. "Spread your legs for me as wide as you can so I can watch your pussy melt when I lick your asshole."

"But what if I'm a bad girl?" I asked.

"Bad girls get a spanking. Is that what you want?"

"You gave Lisa a spanking."

"She told you that? I gave her a spanking because she told me she couldn't feel anything. You know what I'm talking about. I proved her wrong."

"I'll say." I didn't mention that I had *witnessed* the spanking and the fantastically sexy way he had punished her breasts, too. Maybe later.

"Get on your knees and bend over," he growled.

Like a good girl, I did.

He climbed behind me. "You gonna shake it for me, baby?"

I wriggled my ass, anticipating his tongue. He started to kiss my cheeks, exploring those precious mounds with his knowing hands and hungry mouth.

"Relax now, angel. Let's open you up," he whispered, and then his lips landed on my waiting hole, his tongue like a hot little dagger as it darted around that tight, sensitive chasm.

I writhed with pleasure. Robert held me still by gripping my cheeks with both hands, pulling them farther apart as he rimmed me delicately.

Another moan climbed through me. He responded by dipping his tongue inside and fucking me softly a few times. Then he pulled out, circling the sodden edges of my asshole before poking back inside, piercing me more deeply with his tiny cock.

"Tell me you want it," he said.

"I want it," I said with a gasp.

"Tell me how much," he directed.

My naked ass was high in the air. I shook it for him as a mare would shake its mane, and he pet it gloriously before he slid one finger, then two, into my sopping pussy. Expert that he was, he pressed those fingers against the sensitive wall of tissue between my anus and my cunt. I heard the sound of sucking—his mouth on the thumb of his other hand, probably. I waited for it to plunge into my ass.

When it did, I bucked. I felt Robert's breath on my back, making my flesh tingle. He started to pump me with one hand, the fingers probing each hole pushing toward the other.

"Did she fuck you like this?" he asked.

"No."

"Did you fuck *her* like this?" He pushed his thumb deeper inside.

"Yes," I answered.

"You fucked her in the ass?"

"Did you?" I countered.

He answered by doubling the speed of his thrusts. I met them with a long, throaty groan. As he pumped into me, the groan eventually broke into bits, disintegrating into uneven gasps.

"Stay still now," he finally said.

As if I could. Jackknifed, my ass swayed in the air, my thighs quaking. With most of my weight pressing down on my shoulders, I gripped the sheet with both hands, my head on a pillow, my lungs desperate for air.

"I can't." I was breathing so heavily. "More. I need more. . . . "

"That's right, baby. You need *me*. I'm gonna fuck you in the ass now," he whispered. "Give me everything and I'll make it so special."

My ass was already trembling. Yes, I did need him. And I sensed how much he needed me to surrender to him, especially after my being with *her*.

I reached back and pulled my cheeks apart. "Like this?"

He grunted. "That's it, baby. Open up for me. I want you to touch your baby just the way you like it."

I moaned once again as I slid one hand between my legs, through my soaked pussy lips to my enormously swollen, aching bud.

"Ah, that's it," he whispered. "Let me see you love it."

Robert knelt behind me now, pushing my knees farther apart with his own. As I circled my clit with two fingers, he gripped my hips and pulled me against him.

Slowly, he pushed his cock into my secret space.

"Let me in," he insisted.

And I did. Not every woman would or could or even wanted to surrender in this way, but I did. Part of it was relinquishing control, yes. Another part was acknowledging that I wanted to be taken—dominated—in just this way. Part of it, too, was that once those two aspects had washed through me, the intensity of the experience itself took over. There was no room for thought of any kind, not when the cocktail of pain, surprise, and sudden wonder that accompanied the first moments of an ass-fucking translated into complete rapture.

Quite simply, Red, you can be nowhere else but enveloped in that encounter. And just as his dick deepens inside of you, so does the moment. As the initial pain transforms into pleasure, the rest of your life melts away. It feels like you are melting, too, and it is in that sensation that you yourself are transformed, seemingly made anew, the intricacies of life beginning again with each thrust.

My middle finger licked my shining pearl as he started inching into me. I bore down with my knees and tried to let loose, to open for him. My clit somersaulted as the first sensations of sodomy swept through me: fear, abandon, fire, capitulation, want.

"Are you still touching your baby?" he asked.

I grunted in acknowledgment, I had no words left.

"Touch your pussy, too," he directed. "I want to see you drip on the sheets while I fuck you."

I groaned, sliding two fingers to my overflowing hole. I dragged my fingers up and down my slit.

The familiar clap of his balls against my ass added to the swirling sensations that pulsed through my entire being as he plugged me. It felt like I was being torn open, but at the same time, my every synapse begged for *more.*

"Did she fuck you like this?" he demanded.

"Fuck you!" I shouted.

"Oh no, angel, you mean fuck *you* because this is *your* sweet ass that is getting the best fuck you've ever had."

His cock was like a knowing force of nature inside of me, finding all of me, demanding I was completely present. There was no way not to be present as he pounded me, no way not to give everything to him.

"Robert!" I cried.

"Zoey!"

"I love you!"

"I love you more! Feel my cock loving you," he said as he slammed into me. "Feel my balls loving you! You feel me?"

So much feeling roared through me I thought I might lose consciousness.

I gasped, clenching my buttocks as my fingers brushed over my clit and up and down my cunt, as if I were painting myself with my own juices. The instant I felt the familiar stiffening of Robert's entire body, I knew he would climax in a moment. With one final thrust, I pushed back against him.

Imagine a flower opening, Red. Imagine the bloom of it pushing toward the sky with all its might, seeking the dazzling rays of the sun, the mesmerizing light of day, the rapture of the slightest wind. Now push that wind inside my body and feel how it soars through me, lifting the very center of me, finding the mysterious, hidden source of ecstasy that now hurtles through my being, fans across my synapses, blooms through my pussy like that flower sprawling into being.

And don't forget about the rain, the drumming, driving, relentless rain. Thunder, lightning, a tumultuous storm. The sky being torn into an echo of itself.

That was my orgasm. It catapulted through me as I pushed back and clutched Robert. With his last thrust, we both dissolved into the sudden oneness of the universe, a climax of vaporous breath and billowing being, like planets merging. There we collapsed, a singular molecule announcing its ultimate bliss.

We lay like that for a while. No words, just feeling. We touched each other, held the other, uttered satisfied sounds.

But then, because he was Robert, he had to say something.

"Did she fuck you like that?" he whispered.

How could he—why would he?—ask me such a thing after what we had just experienced? It didn't matter; he had. And because of that, I had to show him, prove to him, that he was mine, that he belonged to me.

Red, can you guess how?

I leaned close and kissed him deeply. Then I climbed out of our bed and walked over to the dresser. In the second drawer were the sex toys. I reached for the dildo, the eight-inch black one with the black leather harness, and I watched my husband word-lessly while I stepped into it.

Robert gazed at me with bright eyes.

What did he feel? Wonder? Fear? Both? The same emotions I felt whenever he approached *my* tender little asshole? I did not ask him because I did not want more words—I wanted raw feeling. I reached for the lube and slowly sauntered back over to the bed so that he could watch my dick bob and sway. See how hard I was for him. See how I could fill him up and make him burst. Know how much I wanted him, how much I loved him.

I leapt onto the bed. I landed on my knees and shimmied my hips so that my potent black beast shook, too.

Lying on his back, Robert smiled from coast to coast as I strad-dled his shoulders.

"Okay, bitch," I growled playfully. "I want you to suck my prick before I fuck you. You ready for me?"

He answered by wrapping his lips around my dark animal. I moaned and held his head in my hands as he took more of me into his mouth. I watched with admiration as he ran his tongue along its edges, up and down its sides, pulling it in. I marveled as he suddenly took it in deep, all the way into his throat with a gut-tural groan. The sound reverberated through my beast and al-most made me start to fuck his face with abandon.

I refrained, though, both out of tenderness for my man and because I really wanted to let loose in his ass. We settled into a slow sucking rhythm for a few minutes more as I reached back and began to pull on Robert's own rising pole.

I liked him on his back when I fucked him this way so that I could watch him work his own rod while I rocked him. I also loved to watch his face as I plugged him, because the expressions were unlike any other. First there was a combination of pain and surprise. The pain would melt into pleasure after the first careful strokes, and then the real fucking would begin. The only other times I ever saw his face flush that deep red was when he played sports.

As I slowly pulled out of his mouth, it was obvious that he did not want to let me go. Of course not; he wanted me to get him off with the hand that rode his own hard dick. But it was way too soon for that.

"Be patient, lover," I whispered, kissing him gently before I inched down his torso. I paused at his pecs and took one of his nipples into my mouth. I sucked it until he moaned, then flicked my tongue over it until he panted. After I'd done precisely the same thing to his other bud, I made lazy circles down his belly to his nest. I breathed him in, adoring the musk of him, and kissed his pulsing prick.

"Suck it," he said.

"Good boys say *please*," I whispered.

"Please!" He blurted.

"Later," I said, my breath heaving. "You can't come yet."

He groaned with frustration.

"I know, baby, but I promise I'll make it worth it."

"Promise?"

I nodded. Finally between his legs, I squeezed some lube onto my big black rod. Robert lifted his legs so that I could sit between them, with mine hugging his torso. I lifted his balls and slowly entered him. He grunted and his cock twitched as I slipped my tip inside, waiting for him to relax before going any deeper.

"Touch yourself," I whispered, and he did. One hand wound around his bulging shaft. He worked it slowly as I gently squeezed his sweet balls. When I started to tug them he writhed with pleasure, his ass opening up to me bit by bit. I had at least four inches inside as he slathered his cock with his own juices, which meant I was halfway there.

I watched the expression on his face change from shock to impatience as he waited for the pleasure to kick in, then to bliss as I finally began to pump him. I went deeper with each stroke. His movements matched mine as I rode his ass and he rode his cock.

My black beast came complete with balls, and I felt them pressing against my bud the harder I fucked him. I gyrated my hips as I finally slid all eight inches into his tight hole. The look on his face was the opposite of pain, the promise of ecstasy.

"Zoey!" he cried.

"Robert!" I shouted.

"I love you!"

"I love you!"

I blasted into him then, pumping him as deeply as I could. His hand was like a piston on his prick, and I knew he would come any minute. I squeezed his balls and ground against him. My own black balls punished my clit as he finally arched, his ass grabbing me tightly, and his cum began to spurt.

His entire body shuddered as he milked his cock, and I stopped moving inside of him. The convulsive waves of his orgasm enveloped my dick. They pulsed along my rod and I felt it in my balls, which nestled against my clit. All I had to do was press down and grind—my own climax roared through me.

Robert grabbed my legs as I writhed against him, still inside him, still hard! A final stream of hot milk arced out of him, like a sexy tribute to our love. We both fell back then, sated, connected, complete.

You know what the question was. At that moment, neither one of us asked it.

JAKE

"Zoey and Robert . . . Robert and Zoey . . . Eventually, we told each other every single detail of what we'd done with Lisa. Sometimes we'd act it out, sometimes we'd fuck it away. Like I said, Red, to get fucked is everything. To really get fucked, you give everything. That was how Robert and I were able to forgive each other, reach each other, understand ourselves more completely, and become even closer as a result.

"Lisa had been right: I had taught Robert, and he had taught me. To be open, daring, willing, adventurous. To take sex as lightly as we took it seriously. To always be willing to experience something new, to never be closed.

"And that was why, when we talked about Bali again, we did so with our new favorite four-letter word in mind: Lisa."

Wow, Stella. Life is full of surprises, eh? Especially when it comes to sexuality. Zoey and Robert are obviously tight, but not tight-assed. That was a joke, get it? Okay, you're not wagging. Let's move on. So that was the first letter that came. Now, listen to this:

◆ ◆ ◆

Dear Mr. Shoe,

I'm going to guess that you're a man, and I'm going to guess that you are not wearing red shoes. It was a woman who wore them, wasn't it, the woman who betrayed you? The reason for this ad of yours?

I'm more than happy to tell you my tale, because none of us wants to be alone in our misery, do we? Besides, maybe it'll help.

So here goes.

I'm single, pretty attractive, and addicted to sex. My breasts have always been popular; they've opened many doors for me. And I mean gender doors—they've landed me in the arms of both men *and* women.

I hope you're not judgmental, 'cause that would just be a big drag. Maybe you're a breast man yourself. It seems a lot of people are. And maybe because mine are big—I'm talking 40DD here— they've led the way into a whole new world.

As soon as I realized how strongly people responded to them, I began to use them to my advantage. I was fully developed at twelve, lost my virginity at twelve and a half, and I've never looked back!

The problem is, once you begin to rely on sex to get close to people, you kind of stop getting close to them in other, maybe more real, ways. I say maybe because I don't know. Maybe sex is as close as we can ever get to another person. What do you think, Mr. Shoe?

Besides that, what I'd really like to know is how close you can get to *two* people at once. If you have sex with both of them, does that mean you're inside their relationship? I mean, how can you not be? I'm willing to tell you that I just had that experience and it was astonishing. I don't mean that I had sex with both of them at the same time. No, not a threesome. I had sex with each of them, separately. When I had sex with the husband, the wife was watching. He didn't know it, but I did. So by the time I met the wife, she and I already shared a secret.

The secret he and I shared is that I approached him and I se- duced him. Not necessarily the way it's done, isn't that so? And my own little secret is that I knew he was married, and that's why

I wanted him. I can't be bothered with these guys who want to marry me just 'cause I've got big boobs. That type of guy really bugs me. I mean, just 'cause I've got these magnificent tits doesn't mean I don't have a brain. Ask his wife and you'll understand.

I knew she was watching us from the moment I laid eyes on her in the club. She didn't know I knew, but that's why I suggested we go to a motel. I knew she'd follow, and she did. That night, I performed as much for her as I did for him. It was a real turn-on.

Then I went back to the club every night for the next several nights. I knew she would show up sooner or later, and she did. Dressed like a *man*. That was clever, but not clever enough. She was too beautiful to be a guy. I could see right past her cute disguise, but I let her play it out, and only after I had wooed her with my, shall we say, charms, did I expose her.

And expose her I did. To the tune of her naked on her back, her legs spread wide before me, her pussy dripping as she begged me to fuck her.

And fuck her I did! Mr. Shoe, have you ever fucked a virgin? Well, that's a silly question; I imagine that chances are you have. What I mean is, have you ever fucked someone who's never been fucked by someone of her own sex? It's incredibly exciting when they realize what they've been missing. In a word, it's phenomenal.

And that's what she was like. When I fucked her. When she fucked me. When he fucked me. When I fucked him.

Him. Her. Me.

How about him, her, me, and you?

Come on, Mr. Shoe. Don't tell me my little tale hasn't turned you on. . . .

P.S. A personal little tidbit for you. Have you ever thought of how phallic, aside from erotic, it is to paint a woman's lips with a sexy shade of lipstick? Try Rampant Red next time. Red lipstick on a woman is a dangerous thing. Kisses to you. . . .

Rampant Red, huh? Do you think she'd let me paint her . . . Hmmm, maybe I'll write her back. What would I tell her, Stella? Truth, sex, or lipstick. Which is the most amazing healer? Bark once for truth, twice for sex, and three times for . . . Oh, so now you're wagging that tail of yours. I get it.

Talk to Me, Baby

♦

that's how I h...
want to g...

JAKE

Stella, I think it's been good for us—the move to the beach, I mean. It's not like I can let go of my entire past, but I can try to live in the here and now, right? At the very least, we're ahead of the game with our daily beach runs. I mean, just listen. This one's from St. Bartholomew's Hospital, Lancaster, California. . . .

Hmm. I hope it's not serious.

♦♦♦

Dear Lonely Boy,

Please excuse the stationery and my wobbly handwriting. Seems I broke my thumb. But other than that and a slight concussion, they tell me I'm okay. No surprise nothing happened to Bud—nothing ever does. Bud's my boyfriend, my main squeeze, my sex toy. Of course, they *did* end up barring him from the hospital for trying to make love to me in the emergency room. So

...ave come to write to you. Anyway, you probably
...t right down to the juicy stuff, so here goes. . . .

Bud and I love to hear a good house band, but last Saturday the band didn't show up. At the last minute, the management had to scramble to put out some kind of entertainment. So . . .

"It's chitlin' time!" is what the M.C. shouted as we walked in. Onstage, four women paraded around in soaking wet T-shirts.

"Okay, ladies, turn around for everybody!" he called. "Look at them, folks. All natural, organic, not a scalpel mark on one of 'em. . . . !"

True to form, Bud grabbed my hand and lunged toward an empty table as close to the stage as he could get. No sooner had we sat down did he bolt up to his feet and start hollering at one of the chicks:

"You! Hey, darlin'! You, you're the one! I tell you, you're the one, baby!"

An instant later, the M.C. called out, "And the winner is . . ."

"You're the one!" Bud shouted.

". . . Regina!" the M.C. announced.

You guessed it, you lonely thing. Bud had been creaming over Regina! The crowd started cheering, and Bud could not contain himself:

"Regina, you're number one, darling! You're it! Whoa!"

That was enough. I grabbed him and made him sit down. I mean, come on, he's supposed to be spending Saturday night with *me*, the jerk.

Meanwhile, the M.C. was cheering her on as she paraded around with her completely drenched big tits.

"Regina!" the M.C. shouted. "Shake it, baby!"

And she did.

"Regina!" Bud butted in. "Hey, you, yeah darling! Honey! Honey, you're the winner! No doubt, right?"

He turned to the crowd. "She's the winner, right? Number one. Numero uno, right? Yeah, no doubt about it!"

Lonely Boy, that was it for me. I'm used to his shenanigans— basically he can barely keep it in his pants, and that's what keeps him in *my* pants. But this was just *stupid*.

Let him go fuck the chick, and I'll find my own good time tonight. I reached for my purse and stood up to go.

Like the child that he is, he grabbed me.

"Where you going?" he barked. "It's a contest. I'm just votin'. This is America! I was just expressin' an opinion."

"Later, baby," I replied. "I've got other ships to sail." I shook him off of me and strode away toward the restroom.

Give Bud a couple of beers and anything can happen. But when he goes too far, I usually yank the leash and reel him in. Not tonight, though. He wants to have his cake and eat *me*, too? I'm just not in the mood to be his last course tonight.

As I walked away, the M.C. climbed onto the stage and grabbed Regina's hand.

"Regina! Let's hear it out there!" he called out. "C'mon, let's make some noise!"

I didn't look back. I was sure that Bud had bounded up yet again.

As I walked toward the bathroom, Ms. Big Tits herself started talking. If you ask me, she should have kept her mouth shut.

Regina began, "I'd like to thank my parents . . . and my ex-boyfriend . . . and Dr. Katz . . ."

Dr. Katz? For those monstrous tits, I imagine.

I saw Bud heading to the bar for another beer.

"And all you guys who voted for me . . . And now, something for the boys."

I turned to see her cup her crotch moments before I entered the bathroom.

"Oh, yeah . . . remember, boys . . . I'm Regina, from North Carolina! Conserve water. Don't drink and drive. Just say no. And practice safe sex!"

As I opened the door, the M.C. announced:

"No, no, no . . . ladies and gentleman, I'm going to predict that not one single solitary soul here tonight will be forgetting Regina . . . from North Carolina!"

I turned around as Ms. Wet Tits hopped off the stage and made a beeline for Bud at the bar. She grabbed his crotch as she strode by, walking in the direction of the men's restroom. She stopped at the door and with an incline of her head, invited him in. He wasted no time zipping in after her.

I wheeled around and went into the women's restroom. Immediately, I heard the wet, pumping sounds of sex in one of the stalls directly opposite the mirror. At the bottom of the stall, I saw two pairs of trendy black boots, one behind the other, both pointed toward the wall. Ah, so she was getting it from the back. Whoever it was bent over in there, she was getting fucked—and good!

As I put on fresh lipstick, to my shock and disappointment, I realized I could hear the conversation from the men's bathroom through the wall.

"That's right, baby, tell me I'm number one," Bouncy Tits teased.

"You are *so* number one," Bud replied.

"Say it again . . . numero uno!"

"Numero uno, baby!"

The fucking in the stall behind me got more intense, and its flimsy walls started to shake. At this point, I could only see one pair of feet—I gathered that the fuckee had either wrapped her legs around the waist of her love or was kneeling on the commode as she took the pounding. Her panting deepened into broken groans. As I powdered my face, the stall door suddenly flew open. All I had to do was look in the mirror to see the scene behind me. It was two chicks, and the one on her knees on the closed seat was getting absolutely slammed from behind! The fucker had moved to one side and wrapped her arm around the other one's hips so that she could hold her in place while she rode her with her arm, and I do mean hard! The fuckee was squealing and yelping on her knees as her lover pounded away.

Wow—two chicks doing some major fucking. That was something you didn't see every day. Or maybe I should say, it was something *I* didn't see every day. I have to admit, it was hot. My clit thought so, too. A little slice of lightning zapped it awake, and a sweet ache spread through my pussy as I watched.

When the lover turned her head and saw me, I smiled big. I'm pretty open—at least willing to be open. She smiled back and slowed down her fucking, finally pulling out of her girl's cunt so she could spread her glistening lips. I could see her swollen, deep red slash. Mine pulsed at the sight, and I did not move from the spot where I stood. The fuckee started moaning, and whimpering, wriggling her butt for more.

The lover held her lips open with one hand so that I could see it all. She slid three fingers back into the chick's gushing hole, pumped her a few times, then pulled out. Sliding up to her clit, she circled it slowly. The fuckee shook her ass and started to tremble all over. The lover dove back into her, pumped her a few more times, then slid her fingers slowly back to her clit. By the fourth time she followed this pattern, the fuckee's whole body was shaking. She kept her balance by pressing her palms against the wall, panting the entire time like the animal she clearly was.

After giving me a wink, the lover whispered to her woman, "Cum for me, baby." With three fingers firmly inside, she flicked her thumb up and down the fuckee's clit until her body shook violently, and she let loose an ecstatic cry as she came and came and—no lie—she came.

I swear, I almost lost it from watching. The lover and I smiled at each other once more and then I slipped out the door. Give the girls some privacy, you know.

It dawned on me that I had not heard any more conversation from the men's room. What was going on in there?

Surprise, Lonely Boy. I opened the door to the men's restroom and what did I find but Ms. Winning Tits herself and Bud, sucking face. He was pawing at her dumb fake tits. As she slid to her knees; I watched, unnoticed by them. Bud's eyes were closed, his mouth spilling: " Baby . . . whoa . . . number one!"

For a moment, I took in the scene. She unbuttoned his jeans and the beast that was his dick sprang out. As I retreated, Bud's eyes opened and met my gaze.

Fucking cheat!

On my way out of the club, Bud followed. Still fumbling to zip his jeans, he charged toward me in the parking lot.

"Baby! Where you goin'?" he called. "What are you doin'? C'mon! Nothin' happened! Look, we were just talkin'. Come on!"

As I stood in the parking lot listening to this mouthful of

trash, he started to push me toward the Mustang. I wasn't going to waste my energy fighting him.

That silly lime-green Mustang, his true pride and joy. Though he always said I was his true pride and joy. Like I believed that, especially given what I'd just seen.

Bud opened the passenger side door and tried to push me in.

"Come on baby, get in the car," he pleaded. "Please, baby . . . please."

Lonely Boy, the truth is I did love that car—it was the last of the Boss bad boys. Bud's was a 1970 351, a midblock terror that held its own. Usually it was hard to keep me out of it. But given the circumstances, I made him beg a little before I climbed in. Then he crawled into the driver's side.

"Listen," he said to me, "you can either believe me or believe your eyes! We'll go for a ride and talk about it."

Believe my eyes or believe him? He was always saying ridiculous things like that, words that contradicted, that ultimately made no sense whatever. But idiotic as they were, they strangely endeared him to me. I mean, let's face it, Bud was stone cold dumb, a rock-brained man.

And I loved him.

Who understands chemistry between two people? I don't, and I gave up trying to figure it out a long time ago. I believe that chemistry is the most essential ingredient in a relationship. Not compatibility. Not a good sense of humor. Not shared values and interests. For two people to stay together, it has to be impossible for them NOT to fuck. I call it the Law of Lust. There are all sorts of online dating services promising men and women that they'll find their soul mate based on highly sophisticated psychological questions and personality tests. What crap! It's lust, LB, that's the fuel, the gas and oil that fires the engine of a relationship.

Vroom vroom vroom—that's Bud and me in the bedroom. And that is the main reason he's been my boyfriend for the past two years. Bud and his three-legged rottweiler. His two-ton steel pick-up truck with marshmallow bumpers. Drinking tequila with milk chasers. His long, dark, heavy-metal hair and granite hard muscles. He's a brute puppy with a constant hard-on.

He's a mechanic, works with his hands, and smells like grease and oil at the end of a day's work. He's got calluses on his palms from gripping tools tight—wrenches, pliers, screwdrivers. I had no idea when I met him that lug nuts would turn me on. Horsepower would get me hot. Oil filters would make me wet. Glove compartments would fuel my fantasies. But they do.

And so does Bud, though he can be a real dick. Drinks too much beer. Fucks other women. His brain plays shortstop to the thick dumb bat between his legs that dictates 95 percent of his behavior. So every once in a while he needs the leash strapped on and yanked hard.

I feel particularly qualified to share my views on relationships, Lonely Boy, and I'll tell you why. I own a small lingerie boutique in Santa Barbara that caters to wealthy, slender, ultrafeminine women. Most of my merchandise comes from Paris. I hand select each item. The designs are sophisticated, sexy, with only a few revealing, slightly trashy selections thrown into the mix.

Many of my customers will eventually seek out my advice as to what to buy to keep their boyfriends and husbands turned on.

Invariably they'll want the trashiest teddy, the most lurid thong, and often I feel their almost helpless distress. There's no hint of heat, no lust left in their marriages or relationships, and they're terrified of losing security: home, social status, identity as wife and mother or girlfriend. Will they be replaced by a younger, sexier model? I can't help but see the anxiety in their eyes.

Given the size of the shop, it's hard not to eavesdrop on my customers' conversations. The reality is, many of these dolls spend a lot of time denigrating the very men they're so desperate to hang onto. I often suspect that many of them don't love their husbands or steadies, and maybe never have.

Once in a while they'll ask me if I have a boyfriend.

Yes, I'll reply.

What does he do? (A tired, irrelevant question.)

He's a mechanic.

Then there will be that slight pause filled with judgment, followed by the false response, *Oh, how interesting. Does he work on Mercedes? How handy to have a man that can fix your car.*

What I want to say to them is this:

Bud makes me drip.

He's a fuck machine.

He eats me out at least three times a week.

As far as I'm concerned, Bud could collect garbage or unemployment checks. So what if he's uncouth, uneducated, and even rough at times? So what if he's a few springs short of a total rear leaf? He's got a big dumb heart that matches his big fat dick.

We never get bored. We push each other. Fight for the fun of it. I'll antagonize him just to get him riled up, pissed off, even enraged. Why? F-u-c-k-i-n-g. Simple as that. Nothing like a furyfuck! Ever since we met, we've shoved each other into exploring sex and love without limits. That's why I'm writing to you, Lonely Boy—from my hospital bed—because Bud and I crossed another line in our relationship. Maybe a dangerous, truly insane line, but oh, it was worth it!

I guess you'll have to judge for yourself.

So let's go back to Saturday night. After we were both seated in the Mustang, Bud gunned the gas pedal and we burned rubber onto the highway. Such drama, such flair in how he expressed himself with his wheels. (And these particular wheels, by the way, are stamped steel standard with corporate trim rings and caps. Just letting you in on that, LB. It makes me tingle all over).

"Oh, God!" Bud started. "So you're mad at me? Well, I can understand that. I mean . . . ah, you're right, but just like the counselor says, it's healthy for you to express your anger."

The counselor. Some dime-store shrink we've been seeing 'cuz Bud can't keep his dick in his pants when he sees a hot babe. He's like a dog in heat. Well, I am not his bitch, though I was feeling like one at that moment. I looked out the window, pretending that I had not even heard his comment.

"That's what I like about you!" he went on. "C'mon, it's nothing we can't work out. . . . You give a little, I give a little. No one gets hurt, okay? So let's talk about it. Yeah, okay, so . . . I guess you expect me to explain. All right, so that's good, we're having a discussion. . . ."

My lip was zipped.

"Like I said, we were just talking. She followed me. She found me in the men's room with my pants down. She wouldn't stop talking. Some girls are like that, you know? They just won't take no for an answer. . . ."

Was that right? I hadn't seen any discussion between them earlier, just a lot of ridiculous pawing. I started to hum a little tune, ignoring him completely.

"What was I supposed to do, huh? Put yourself in my shoes. What would you do, huh?"

Not a peep out of me.

"So, okay, you don't want to put yourself in my place. Put yourself in her place, huh? Poor thing, probably never had a compliment before. I felt sorry for her standing there in the back. I can see her right now at home on a Saturday night, watching TV, all alone. Poor thing. Finally she got enough nerve to go out. I felt sorry for her."

So now he was sorry for her. Come on, anyone could do better than that.

"That's right," he echoed. "I felt sorry for her."

Well, if he couldn't even convince himself, how was he going to convince me? I switched on the radio.

He switched it off.

"See? Hell!" he barked. "Sometimes you try to do something nice for someone, and it gets all misinterpreted. You end up in the doghouse. All right," he said with a sigh, "look, baby . . . I admit it. I'm human. . . . I make mistakes like everybody else. I don't have all the answers. Look at me. Look. It's true, I'm shaking. Look at that."

He held out his hand in front of my face.

"Look. You have me pushed up against the wall. I'm shakin'. See? Look. Look!"

I yawned and looked straight ahead. Bud's shiny right fender was headed toward a set of barricades at a construction site on the side of the highway. It slammed into a pair and then the car swerved violently away.

Not a word out of me.

Bud didn't flinch. Had he done it on purpose? I couldn't tell.

"Shit! All right, all right, all right," he went on. "You're right, you're right, it was me. But it wasn't really *me*. . . . It was one of those out of body experiences, you know, like we read in the funny papers on the checkout line at the supermarket. And you know what? It was scary!"

From sorry to scared. I love it. To express my glee, I gave him a quick punch in the arm.

"It was!" he insisted. "It was scary. It was! Come on. You can't do this to me. Not right now. Not when you know how really, really vulnerable I am right now. You know things haven't been going good at work. The economy . . . Smitty just got fired . . . I could be next. People aren't interested in craftsmanship anymore, just as long as their cars start in the morning, that's all they give a shit about. You know, nobody needs a carburetor artist like me anymore. That's right, a good mechanic is an endangered species, just like the dinosaurs. It's just a matter of time before I end up as fossil fuel in someone else's tank. So it's perfectly understandable that when Saturday night comes around, me and guys like me on the verge of extinction need to let off a little steam. Yeah! But you know, the difference between me and them is that I take you with me. I do. Everywhere I go I take you with me, right? We're in it together, right? Right?"

That part was true—he did take me with him. We weaved a bit in our lane, but only a bit. He must have had fossil fuel on the brain to think that witnessing his infidelities in person translated into a special Saturday night for me.

But my lips were sealed.

He sped up, moving across the highway to the exit ramp.

"Talk to me, baby. Please!"

Not one little syllable.

"All right, I'll tell you what. I'll make a deal with you. I'm going to shut up and not even try to deny that something upsetting may have happened back there. But just answer one question: Tell me for the record what would you have done if you were in my shoes? Huh? What would you have done? Tell me!"

I love when he orders me around like that. I switched on the radio again.

He switched it off.

"Goddamn it! You're really starting to piss me off, you know that?" he bellowed. "You know why? Because every time we have an argument you feel like you gotta win!"

We careened around a corner. The momentum caught me off guard, and I fell against Bud. Not missing a beat, he grabbed me and kissed me. I bit his lip and pulled away, leaving blood and lipstick smeared across his mouth.

He banged on the leather-bound steering wheel.

"Damn it, you bit me! God, I hate this! This is stupid! There you are, blaming me for some shit that ain't me!"

Now that was articulate, eloquent, even. *Some shit that ain't me.* My smooth-talking stud.

"My sex drive is in my DNA!" he cried. "It's in my genes! Hell, my old man lost both his legs in the war, and he still has the hottest reputation back home in Tempe. Even with those college kids and everything. He's still numero uno with the ladies! That's right! I said *ladies.* And my brother Delbert, forget about it! The Big D! Say no more!"

Indeed, not one single vowel from me. Oh, he was pumping himself up now.

"Talk about sex drive," he spilled. "What about when you went through that phase when the only way you could get turned on was if we did it in public?"

He laughed. I didn't.

"At football games, eh, with the crowd cheering all around us? Everybody else is blockin' and tacklin' and we're back there fucking? Jesus! God!"

I turned away and looked out my window. Did he think this was getting me hot?

"How about in traffic, huh? When we were stuck in traffic and those truckers were looking down on us? I didn't know what to do! Or in the park, on Sunday afternoons, huh? Remember that? Do ya? How about in the windows of a certain tall building at night with all the lights on?"

He laughed again, even more pleased with himself. I frowned as I stared straight ahead. Didn't stop him.

"God! You remember the Cadillac, don't you? Huh, the Cadillac? Oh, God! Don't tell me you don't remember!"

Not to worry, I wasn't going to tell him anything. I turned my face to the window again, envisioning the red beauty on wheels.

"Remember, the Cadillac in the garage on the lift? While Smitty was changing the oil? Remember we had to be real careful—it started swinging back and forth?"

He laughed again. I bit my lip.

"C'mon, baby, talk to me. . . . Say anything. C'mon. Think about all the good times we've shared together. Think about all the times I've been there for you. Huh? Hmm?"

Hmm, like tonight? I let my seat recline and lifted my feet to his precious dashboard, pressing into it with the sharp heels of my black pumps.

He winced.

"How about that time in Myrtle Beach?" he asked. "We were so goddamn hot I thought I was gonna die. Nine hours straight."

True, we went at it for nine hours straight our first night there. We stayed in one of those high-rise hotels right on the beach, but after a few drinks at the bar, we didn't leave the room until the following morning. The air-conditioning unit broke halfway through the night and the place steamed up, but we were so steamy ourselves it didn't matter.

The thing about Bud is his dick. It's magnificent. Really. Unbelievably beautiful. Sweet and pink and clean, all eight thick, hard inches of him. And, I should add, full of surprises. The way that hot rod (and I do mean *hot rod*, Lonely Boy) fits in my box is indescribable. It's really exactly that—that he fits. And his balls, they are like a perfect, tiny little ass bound by his cock ring. I love to nibble them when he's watching a game, make him moan when he's pretending that I'm bothering him—he's so invested in whatever side he's rooting for, you know. Are all guys like that, LB? What is it with guys and sports? Is it the only place they get to touch each other, even smack each other's asses, and not freak out? Is that it? Seems that way to me. Anyway, Bud is either flat on his back or reclining in his favorite La-Z-Boy chair when a game is on. I like to tease him then, knowing he's too involved with the game to get with me at that moment, but that I can still get him hard, despite his protests.

Back in Myrtle Beach that first night, the only game he was into was *me*. One of his fantasies is that I'm a whore, which means he's paying cash for me and I'm supposed to do whatever he wants. I'll parade around in various pieces of lingerie, he'll choose my ultimate outfit, and then we'll get down to the nasty. I will totally submit to him in those moments—any position he wants, any place he wants it.

Last time I played Tits-on-a-Stick he had me on my knees on the edge of the tub, him slamming his cock into me and me crying, "Harder, harder," just the way he likes it. After he came he crawled into the tub and had me pee on him. Lonely Boy, have you ever peed on somebody? It gives you a strange sense of power, and it is amazingly intimate. Another thing he likes—no surprise—is role-playing. We've done the classic cheerleader, schoolgirl, mommy (both good and bad), teacher, and rape (both stranger and date).

Actually, it was a rape scene that first night in Myrtle Beach. After we arrived, we went down to the bar and pretended to meet each other for the first time. I played the innocent small-town gal and he played, well, Bud. I wore a short red dress and he wore his usual tight jeans. At least his T-shirt was clean. When he invited me up to his room, of course I said no. But then he began to ply me with booze—my favorite, margaritas—and after three of those, I relented and allowed him to escort me to his (our) room.

At first, he was very gentlemanly. He took my arm, and we walked to the elevator like we were walking down the aisle. Can you see it, Lonely Boy? In the elevator he stepped close and started to run his hands through my hair, whisper sweet things about how special I was and how much he wanted to make love to me. He kissed my cheek very tenderly and then traced my face with his fingertips. Completely sweet. He began to kiss my neck as the elevator doors opened and we stumbled out. He wrapped his arms around me and we danced our way to his room. Utterly romantic.

The thing is, Bud can't really hold back. So once we got inside, all that sweet romance disappeared and in its place, Bud the big stud emerged. After one long, luscious, deep, I-wanna-fuck-you-so-bad kiss, he immediately reached for my breasts.

"No," I said, and tried to push his hands away.

But Bud is strong, obviously. Makes his living with his hands. Instead of pulling away, he gave each of my breasts a healthy squeeze.

I slapped his paws this time. "NO, I said!"

But that only turned him on more. His hands squeezed my tits more tightly beneath my red dress.

"Come on, baby. Give 'em to me. You know I luv 'em. First thing 'bout you I saw downstairs. How perky they are, how juicy."

I hit him again, in the chest. He laughed. The more I struggled, the more he held on, pinching my nipples until they popped hard.

"Ouch!" I said. "You're hurting me. Quit it!"

"Quit it! Quit it!" he taunted. "Baby, I have barely even begun!"

By now he held each breast firmly by the nipple, pulling me closer to him. The more I struggled, the harder he pinched.

"Fuck!" I said.

"Exactly," he said. "You're in no position to tell me what to do, are you, bitch?" He gave my nips another pinch.

"Ow!" I yelped. I kicked his calf.

He didn't flinch. He smiled.

"Don't you wanna play nice? You should do what I tell you to or Daddy might have to spank you hard. You gonna be my good little girl?"

"Fuck you!" I spat.

He released one of my breasts and reached up and around, grabbing a handful of hair so that my neck was completely exposed.

"And . . . oh baby . . . how I'm gonna fuck you back," he whispered. He pulled me close and began to nibble my neck—rough, not tender.

"Grab my cock or I'll bend you over and spank you right now, with my belt. Kick me again and I'll slap your ass silly."

Fuck. I froze.

"Your choice," he crooned, and he twisted my nipples beneath his touch.

I groaned and grabbed his stick. No surprise, it was hard as a steel bolt. In spite of the situation, my clit throbbed.

Fuck.

"That's right," Bud said. "Unzip me." He squeezed my nips.

Ouch. I did.

His big beast sprang out, raring to go. I circled it with my hand just the way he liked it, started stroking.

"Mmm, that's it," he whispered. "Spread your legs wide or I'll ram it in right now."

I spread my legs.

"Are you wet for me, whore?" he asked. "Do me slow. I wanna make it last when I shove it into you."

He released one of my breasts and reached between my legs roughly, ripping my panties away and plunging two fingers into me as he twisted my nipple.

I groaned. Why did it feel so good?

"Good girl," he growled. "Dripping wet for me. Oh, I am gonna fuck you so fucking hard you are gonna feel like I am splitting you wide open. I knew you were a slut from the second I saw you at that bar."

My breath was heavy, and his dick was getting harder as I worked it. His fingers were like pistons in my engine. It was difficult to keep standing.

"Got you all hot and bothered, huh, bitch?" he said. He finally released my sore, stinging breast, and I reached down to squeeze his balls, hard.

"Fuck!" he cried, pulling out of me and then shoving me onto the bed behind us with one big push.

"Now you're gonna get it!"

He leapt on top of me before I could roll away. His full weight upon me, he struggled completely out of his jeans.

"Spread your legs or I'll stick it up your ass right now."

I spread my legs.

"Good bitch. Here I come. . . ."

With one perfect thrust, he was deep inside me.

"Ah . . ." a moan spilled out.

He groaned as he started to pump me, each stroke like a fucking steel rod hitting the very end of me.

I was panting.

"Take it, bitch. Just the way you like it, huh?"

"Nooooo . . ."

"Yes!" he spat. "You are my whore and I am going to fuck you, fuck you, fuck you!"

"NO!" I cried.

He thrust faster and drilled into me. The wet, slapping sound of flesh upon flesh filled the room.

"Fuck you, pussy," he growled. "I'm gonna shoot into you. . . . I'm gonna make you my slut, and you're gonna love it! Tell me you love it. . . . Tell me!"

"NO!"

He grabbed my breasts and squeezed. "Tell me!"

"Fuck!" I cried.

"That's right, bitch. I'm gonna come deep in your cunt. I'm gonna squirt every last bit of juice deep inside you."

With the weight of him completely on me, he ground against my clit. Flashes of pleasure shot through me.

I moaned again. I could feel his orgasm building, rising, about to burst.

"Oh fuck, here it comes. You cunt . . . fuck me . . . fuck me . . . fuck fuck fuck!"

I squeezed the walls of my cunt as he bellowed and burst.

"Ohhh yeah, fuck . . ."

He fell on top of me, gasping.

I held him tight.

"Your turn," he finally whispered. "I'm gonna drink you till you cry."

As you might guess, LB, Bud lived up to his promise . . . and then some. But back to Saturday night.

"That's right," Bud went on. "I said nine hours straight. I kept looking over at the clock and staring at it and thinking to myself, Jesus H. Christ, we're still going at it, I mean nine hours! Straight!"

I slipped off my pumps, stretching my toes slowly.

"A new world's record! Even now when I'm sitting at the house, all alone by myself, I start thinking about it."

There it was, that look in his eye. I knew he'd be quiet at least for a minute or two. We had turned onto a two-lane, tree-lined street. It ran parallel to the highway and had far less traffic. Bud could relive a few more of those memories from Myrtle Beach, and so could I.

At certain moments, life can be very simple. A moment filled with cunnilingus is one of them. Oral sex is one of my favorite things in the world. Bud, lover boy that he is, is enormously gifted at it.

After our nine-hour extravaganza, we both passed out. Late the next morning, I was awakened by a certain something between my legs: Bud's beautiful tongue. As I lay on my back, he licked my inner thighs very slowly. As I stirred, he moaned and parted my legs even wider. With my eyes still closed, I reached down and petted his hair. He responded by trailing his tongue up toward my sleepy—and sore, but oh, LB, in the best possible way—pussy and then dragged it down my leg again with the back of his tongue, all the way to that tender place behind my knee.

He knew that place drove me crazy, so he took full advantage of his knowledge by kissing it gently, and then licking across it, just at the bend, where it was most sensitive.

I moaned, my fingers softly tugging his hair. He flicked his tongue back and forth, and I could not stop my hips from shimmying as my snatch bolted awake, a surge of desire spiraling through me. I arched back, which made him grunt with pleasure, and then he moved his mouth to my other leg, licking slowly up, down, behind, bending my knee so that I could really feel the sweet spot.

"Mmmmm," I said, breathing heavily.

"Mmmmm," he responded.

Dragging his fingers up and down my thighs, he parted them as wide as he could. This way he could watch my pussy lips part, too, and I heard that special grunt he made whenever he saw my gash after an absence. In this case it was probably fewer than six hours, but that's my Bud!

He inched up to my snatch, pushing the lips apart gently with his thumbs to get a good look, and then licked downward directly to my perineum, another of my most sensitive places. Oh, he knew just how to ride me, and I could feel the juices seeping out of me.

He held me open with either hand on the back of each thigh, causing my whole butt to tip up into the air.

"Fuck me with your tongue!" I shouted. Those were my first words on this new glorious day.

Bud groaned. He dipped his tongue into the crack where my asshole lived. I writhed, which made him do it again. He shifted his grip so that his hands could spread my ass cheeks apart, his tongue darting to that amazingly sensitive spot. You guessed it again, Lonely Boy—way responsive spot number three (to say nothing of my tits and my slash, but we've already been there).

He paused at my asshole.

"Fuck me!" I cried, bucking as he flicked his tongue against it. Then he licked up and down my crack, my perineum, stabbing my hole. He moved up to hover above my clit.

"Please!" I called. But that only made him sail his tongue back down to my ass. He pressed it flat against me for a few seconds, and then started swirling it around the edge in circles.

"Ohhhhhhhhhhh!" I cried. I bucked against his hands as he soaked my opening with his saliva. I gyrated even more as he circled it faster with the tip of his tongue.

It was so hot, the way he held me in place and worked my ass. I couldn't help but take one hand from his handful of hair and start to touch my aching clit. He slid his thumb and index finger up to the edge of my hole and parted it so that his tongue could glide in.

"Mmmmm," came from me.

"Mmmmmmmm," came from him, vibrating through my entire being. He held me down and began to drive his tongue inside, in the way only he knew how to. I pushed up against him, wanting to hold him there, keep him inside.

Sweet cream was billowing out of my pussy as I touched myself and panted. Bud slipped two fingers to the entrance to my secret well and plunged them in to the knuckles. I gasped as he pulled them almost all the way out, and then drove them back in. "Stab me, poke me, make me," I wanted to say, but there were no words anymore—just amazing feeling.

As if on cue, Bud pulled away. I was lying there heaving, throbbing, wanting so much for him to lick me to ecstasy. He knew me too well, it seemed, because what he did then was press the thumb of one hand against my titillated little asshole while he slid his tongue up to my throbbing clitoris.

"Baby . . ." I managed.

"Mmmmm," he replied, slipping his fingers back inside as he lowered his mouth onto my clit, wrapping his lips around it in his absolutely perfect, even majestic way.

Yes, my Bud is full of gifts—and this was one of his best. He flicked the tip of his tongue against the center of my universe, and then flicked it again, maybe a dozen, a hundred, a thousand times until I bucked and writhed and hollered as his fucking expert tongue thrashed me to yet another spectacular fucking climax.

Oh, the memory throbbed through me.

The car was flying along the road, all 330 bhps at 5400 rpms going full out, reminding me of my guy.

Bud grunted with satisfaction. "Yeah, baby, we did it all! Everything, every position invented by man or God. Ah, baby!"

And that brings to mind that couple in Ft. Lauderdale. Let's not forget Ft. Lauderdale. What I love about strip poker is even when you lose, you win!"

We lost all right. Bud confused the jack (he thought it looked more like a woman because of the long hair) with the queen and thought he had three queens. Don't forget, Lonely Boy, he's a few spark plugs short of a stacked engine.

The other couple was Cecilia and Larry. We had met them that morning at the hotel's pool. They had a thriving home business where she would masturbate in a variety of costumes on a live Web cam show that he shot and produced. Apparently they raked in a lot of money. She was sexy—all American, honey-blond hair, freckles, and a buff cheerleader's body. Although in her late twenties, she could easily have passed for fifteen. Larry kept the buzz cut he'd had when he was in the Marines and had an equally innocent, boyish face. He was shorter than Bud, but ripped, and his manner was reserved, though there was an obvious playful streak in him that was endearing. And, like Bud, he liked his beer.

When they described their business, Bud kept elbowing me, suggesting that we could do the same thing. All I had to do was give him "the look" and he knew there was no way I was going to sell my pussy on the Internet. Besides, I loved my store. If he wanted to palm his salami for some fast cash, fine.

By the time we reached the end of our strip poker fest, Bud was completely naked except for his socks. I still had on my thong and bra. Cecilia hadn't lost one hand and Larry wore only his boxers and a T-shirt. We all were tipsy; though we'd just met, the booze bonded us as if we'd been friends since high school.

"So, Cecilia, I'd . . . uh . . . love to see you perform," Bud stammered. He tossed Larry a beer. "Dude, only if you don't mind."

It was obvious that Larry was attracted to me and because Cecilia was so at ease, he didn't have to hide it. Each time I stripped off a piece of clothing, his eyes popped wide and a loopy grin crept across his face.

Larry took a long swig of suds. "Bud, you got yourself one fine woman." He turned to me. "Sorry, ma'am, is that offensive?"

"No," I cooed, "maybe I'll perform for you and Cecilia can perform for Bud."

"Cool," Cecilia said.

The guys winked at each other as if they'd just won a race. Men are so predictable at times.

Cecilia began stripping off her clothes. "Actually," she said, "I wouldn't mind trying out some new material for all of you. I've been adding dance to my routine."

The guys plopped down on the couch. I purposely sat on the floor, sliding in between Larry's legs. Bud twitched a bit, but recovered quickly as Cecilia slipped off her panties and revealed a completely shaved pussy, not a single pubic hair in sight. It was a soft pink color with a rouge slit, and her labias were like a pair of tiny pom-poms. I thought Bud's eyes were going to leap off his face.

Personally, I like having a nice bush. I find it sexy and more mysterious, and for me, more womanly. I also have a passion trail that starts below my belly button, a few wisps of dark hair that lead to my muff. I see it as the red carpet that delivers one to my Oscar.

I glanced at Bud's crotch and saw his package already thickening. Remember, Lonely Boy, he wasn't wearing anything but his socks. He caught me looking and quickly slipped a pillow onto his lap.

Cecilia put on a CD. The song that started to play was exotic and soulful, sung by a woman in Portuguese.

"I love Mexican music," Bud chimed.

"Portuguese," Larry and I corrected.

Cecilia turned away from us, swaying her hips and parting her legs. She bent over and wriggled her ass languidly to the rhythms.

Behind me, Larry moved forward and I leaned back so that I could feel his cock beneath his boxer shorts squirm against the back of my neck.

With her hands on the floor, Cecilia literally upended into a headstand. She then spread her legs into a wide "V" position, and her firm, bowl-shaped breasts began to undulate to the beat just as her ass did.

Amazingly, she then held her body in this position with one hand as she slid her other hand between her legs. I have to admit I was getting wet, ocean wet, watching her and feeling Larry's eager, blooming prick against my neck. I looked over at Bud, and I had to smile as the pillow on his lap rose and jiggled.

Still perched on her head, Cecilia licked her fingers seductively then caressed her red button with her middle finger. She parted her slick pom-poms with the others, which revealed her sweet, bald pussy completely. As the first song ended, she rolled onto the floor, her ass facing us, her fingers gliding into her now dripping hole.

All three of us moaned in unison, my own hand inching down my passion trail to my sweet pulsing pussy.

And the Oscar goes to . . .

She was good. Now she blazed a path with her magical fingers between her clit and her tender, pink-puckered asshole. Our heavy breathing, the luxurious music, combined with Cecilia's obvious gift made me feel feverish and frantically horny.

I sat up and asked Larry to unfasten the clasp on my bra. Slipping it off, I grasped my own mounds and squeezed them together. I slid to the floor just as Cecilia began to crawl toward Bud, who whipped the pillow off his lap and flung it across the room.

I turned my attention to Larry, who rose and stepped in front of me. I reached up and pulled down his boxers. Lonely Boy, what a vision waved there. Larry was hung—I swear, this Marine had a tank between his legs. Luckily, Cecilia was already in Bud's lap, her ass dribbling like a basketball, giving him a fantastic ride.

I felt it was my patriotic duty to take the missile before me into my mouth. I got up on my knees, grasped his ass cheeks, and swallowed this Marine whole. He groaned as I worked my mouth up and down his hard shaft, his hands sliding through my hair.

There are no words to describe what it was like to have this mouthful of masculinity pressing against the back of my throat. I mean, this cock should win an award or be donated to the Smithsonian. Believe me, I've had a lot of dick and seen all shapes and sizes even in the ridiculous porn that Bud is addicted to, so I know what I'm talking about.

I held the base of Larry's weapon in one hand and massaged his sack with the other. Wet smacking sounds, Bud's familiar groans, Cecilia's soft squeals, and Larry's pleasure-filled hum resounded in my ears. The music took a back seat to the opus of sex we played with our respective instruments.

Larry's thighs began to tremble. He was losing his balance, so I reluctantly gave up my buffet. He grabbed my hands, that loopy grin as wide as the Atlantic, and pulled me to my feet. He guided me to the other side of their hotel room.

"I like to come in from behind," he said softly. "That cool?"

Bombs away, I thought, it's finally time for the nasty! I leapt on the bed, got up on all fours, and lifted my ass to him. "Bring it on, stud."

My gash was seeping and up to the challenge. Bud's hot rod is big, but this was going to be more meat in my oven than I'd ever dreamed of. I shimmied my hips as he entered me, clutched the blanket in my grip, and pushed my face into the pillow to mute the ecstatic scream that blasted out of me. Larry slapped my ass playfully, not too hard but just enough to dissipate the delirious pain in my pussy. He kept spanking as he reached his free arm around my body. His fingers began circling my swollen nub. Even if this killed me, split me wide open, or I lost consciousness and fell into a coma, I would be one happy fucking girl.

Fuck!

He rocked us as he pummeled my slit. Supersize me, baby, all the way. Bud and Cecilia no longer existed. All that mattered was Larry's tank storming my wicked, wanting barracks. The bed smacked against the wall, and I began pounding it with my fists, "More! More! More!" I cried.

"Yeah! Yeah! Yeah!" Larry grunted like a drill sergeant.

He now worked his fingers hard against my clit, and I could feel my orgasm about to explode. Again, I buried my face in the pillow and wailed, shuddering and quaking, as his rocket erupted and what felt like a quart of hot semen shot into me.

He collapsed on the bed beside me, our bodies slick with sweat, our breathing rough and ragged. Eventually I regained a sense of reality just in time to hear Bud's familiar howl of ecstasy and Cecilia's lusty cries.

Larry rose to go to the bathroom and returned with a towel wrapped around his waist. Prancing over, Cecilia wrapped herself around him. The guys had another beer and then we all said our good-byes.

Back in our hotel room, Bud peppered me with questions

about the size of Larry's penis. I was evasive, but told Bud nobody compared to his hot rod. This was one secret I planned to keep.

The Mustang hummed along, the suspension so smooth thanks to the .85 front sway bar. The road was pretty deserted. Bud liked the back roads because he dug how the 351 took the turns. He'd gun the engine and the rear wheels would spin out with a long *screeeeeech*.

"Then there was the time in Daytona Beach, with that girlfriend of yours. What was her name, Rita? Oh my God in heaven!"

Ah, Rita. Lovely, unexpected Rita.

"You know, when I invited her to our room for a beer, I really thought that'd be it. But she just kept hanging around. And when she wanted to take that shower and asked you to come in and soap up her back . . ."

Nobody was more surprised than me.

"Oh my God! I thought I was gonna bust right then! Hey, it was just so obvious she was hot for you. I'm like, 'Baby, if you want her, you gotta take me, too. It's a package deal.' And she went for it! Oh, man it was so hot!"

I would never disagree with that. Bud and I were vacationing in Daytona Beach, otherwise known as the World Center of Racing—which meant we went to a ton of NASCAR races. So fucking hot, all that burning rubber and roaring testosterone!

After a few days, I decided to give Rita a call. We'd known each other since high school, but had rarely gotten to see each other after we'd graduated. We were too busy with our lives and careers, of course. She was now a captain on a local charter boat out of Ponce

Inlet, a fishing village a bit south of where we were staying. She sounded so happy when I called, so I immediately suggested lunch. Just a little outdoor café called Take the Bait, nothing fancy.

She looked great—sleek and sexy with her straight black hair and laughing eyes and her strong swimmer's legs. She wore a simple sleeveless blue dress. It surprised me when she kissed me full on the mouth as we said, "Hello," but I attributed that to her eager attitude. Silly me! I was startled even more when she started playing footsie with me under the table, but then I finally realized that she was flirting with me. Bud had no idea. When he excused himself to go to the bathroom, I turned to Rita.

I can still feel the embarrassed smile on my face.

"You're flirting with me, aren't you?" I asked.

She giggled. "I can't help it. You're so hot. . . ."

"What? Really?"

"Really. I've always had . . . feelings about you, you know."

"No, I didn't know. You mean, you're . . ."

"I'm bi," she said cutting me off. "And Bud is *hot*, but you are so much *hotter*."

I blushed, never having had a woman say that to me before. It was odd, but that didn't mean it didn't feel good.

She smiled at me full on.

"Well, thanks . . ." I managed.

She reached over and touched my bare forearm. "Do you think there's any possibility that you'd be interested?"

The directness of her question and her light caress made me tingle all over. Of course I'd thought about what it would be like to be with a woman every once in a while, but here was an open invitation. Lonely Boy, you haven't forgotten that Cecilia and I didn't go near each other in Ft. Lauderdale, have you?

"You mean in . . . you and me getting together?" I asked.

She nodded. "Just for now. I'd love to make love to you—and then Bud can join us if you like."

"Really? Just like that?"

She wrapped the perfectly manicured, red-painted fingers of the hand that touched me around my arm. "I've wanted you since high school. It makes me so wet just to say that out loud."

I had to admit, my skin was warming up where she touched me. I didn't know what to say. I had no doubt that Bud would accept her invitation in an instant. But would I?

"We can go really slow," she whispered. "I do know what would make you feel good, I think."

At this point she was rubbing her hand slowly up and down my forearm. Oh yes, that felt good. There it was: the Law of Lust. I smiled, both embarrassed and excited now.

She smiled back, opening her lips and slowly licking the top one from side to side with her tongue. My clit pulsed as if she had just licked *me*.

Can you imagine, LB? I suddenly felt like I'd been living in a box, as if I'd been walking around with my eyes closed in regard to the entire world of women.

Especially Rita. Her hidden sexuality. Her unspoken desire.

Rita must have noticed the dawning on my face, for she slid her tongue over her lip again.

My clit throbbed.

Fuck.

I reached for her, my hand closing over the one she rested on my arm. I squeezed it. She squeezed back. I wriggled in my seat, and she laughed, her bright eyes teeming with delight.

"I'm so thrilled you're not close-minded. You never were," she said.

I didn't know about then, but now I sure wasn't. From the

mere sight of her tongue on her lips I had such a strong reaction. Could I imagine that tongue on my wide-awake clitoris? The answer was definitely, yes.

Bud returned, an interesting—or interested, I should say—expression crossing his face when he saw the two of us sitting close together and touching that way. It was a combination of little boy Bud, setting eyes on his first sports car, and big boy Bud, wanting to play with that hard stick shift between his legs.

"Well, little ladies . . ." He grinned. "Can I get you anything else? Maybe Rita would like to join us in our room for a beer?"

Rita and I burst out laughing. When she immediately agreed to Bud's invite, my clit started to dance. The walls of my pussy undulated, too, like the back-up members in an erotic band.

As you can imagine, Lonely Boy, Bud's Mustang left tracks as he raced back to our room. You know, I love cars. And just then, I loved them even more. All I had to do was sit back and relax. Rita and I sat in the backseat like giddy schoolgirls. She reached for my hand and sidled up close to me like some kind of sexy feline. Her leg pressed against mine like smooth silk. Poor Bud was drooling in the rearview mirror so much he could barely keep from swerving all over the highway. I had to remind him a few times to keep his eyes on the road. There was absolutely no point in getting us all killed before we got back.

When we were almost there, Rita leaned in close and started to whisper to me a fantasy she said she'd always had about me ever since Phys. Ed. class back in high school. We had to change in and out of our uniforms for the sports we were required to play. Our lockers just so happened to be across from each other's in the same aisle.

According to Rita, after my shower I would wrap my towel around my shoulders, and strut—not walk, but strut!—back to my locker. That meant that my ass, and everything else below my belly button, was visible. At that moment, I vaguely remembered that I used to towel dry my hair before air blowing it and that's why I kept the towel around my shoulders. I had no idea that Rita, or any of my other female classmates, was looking at any other part of me.

And that was why, when we got back to our room, Rita wanted to shower and asked me to soap her back for her. In the meantime, she kept telling me her fantasy. I'll let her tell it in her own words, Lonely Boy, so you can really get the picture of how I must have felt hearing it:

"I want to make you feel beautiful. I want you to feel what I feel when I look at you. Your beauty, how it stops my breath, floods through the rest of me. When the water touches your skin, it will be warm and inviting—just like my fingers, how they'll touch you. As the water drips down your body I'll be jealous, because it will get to cover more of you at once than my hands possibly can. So we'll pair up, the water and I. I'll stand behind you and soap you up, then the water will rinse you clean.

"You'll be wet all over, obviously, but I wonder how wet you'll be between your legs as I massage your shoulders and the long muscles of your back, your hot little belly, your luscious hips, paying special attention to that magnificent ass of yours. Maybe I'll drop the soap and you'll bend over to pick it up for me? That would be so sweet, a lovely invitation to slip my hand between your thighs and cup your pussy, holding it gently as you push back against my hand, silently asking me to feel how drenched you are.

"Of course it will be my pleasure, but with only my middle finger, sliding to the place where your desire is seeping out, barely caressing you there, only enough for your nectar to coat a few fingers, your wetness thicker—yes, juicier—than the water itself. Just then, I will not be so envious of the water, for only I will hold your passion in my hand. The water will be unable to.

"After teasing you there, my fingers will slip to your clitoris, really to introduce myself, and then back to your streaming lust. I will do that a few times, so that you can feel me, feel how much I want you. I may bend down and introduce my mouth to your glorious ass, cover it with dripping kisses, linger around the edge of that sweet, secret hole, let my tongue languish in the rain that is falling there.

"By then, beautiful one, I imagine you'll be breathing a little heavier, and I'll help you stand up and turn around to face me. I'll pull you in close and let my naked moist warmth tell you just how much it means to me to feel you this way, completely exposed and vulnerable and wanting. I will run my fingers through your hair, over your face, down your back, across your ass, up your sides, traipse softly along your arms, meet your hands, lift them to my lips. I will kiss each finger and suck the tips gently, slipping them in and out of my mouth as if they are little cocks. Each lick of my tongue will rush directly to your aching clit. When I'm done, I'll lift both your hands to rest on my shoulders, and I will lift mine to your breasts, slowly cupping each tender mound in my hand.

"Your grip will tighten on my shoulders—you're both anxious and excited, not knowing how much pleasure I can bring you. You're used to a man's touch. Yet as my fingers uncurl and begin to caress the soft handful of flesh, a moan escapes you. It seems I know just how to touch them exactly how you like, in precisely the way you touch yourself. Surprise, my darling—that is what it is to feel a woman's touch.

"'Ahhhhhh.' A sigh will leave your lips as I lightly trace the rosy circles of the halos surrounding your nipples. Are your nipples as sensitive as mine, a cord of pleasure twining through the nerve endings that climb down to my clit, sending arrows of deepening sensation with each touch? From the way you bend your head back, beginning to moan and squeezing my shoulders tighter as I touch each one this way, I think so.

"You can't know how long I have fantasized of this dream, or how truly thrilling it is to me to experience your exquisite flesh, to watch you surrender to your pleasure, to know that it is because of *my* touch that you are responding this way. Have you ever wanted something so much, but then become afraid of that very want for fear of the disappointment you know you'll feel in its absence? I have felt this way about you forever, it seems. And here you are, your breathing more like panting, your hands on my shoulders eventually forgetting to squeeze, your nipples completely hard, poking out at me as if searching for more, my fingers slowly beckoning your desire to show more of itself.

"You sigh as I suddenly take my touch away completely. The sound you make is full of surprise and loss. You tilt your head forward and look into my eyes, the water still raining down over us. Your mouth is open and I pull you close, my arms wrapping around you as our breasts mash together and the droplets of water complete us, connect us, envelop us in this steamy, spectacular moment.

"And I haven't even kissed you yet.

"I reach back and turn off the spray. As I do, your hands begin to explore me, sliding from my shoulders down my sides, nestling around my hips as you pull me to you. I moan as you press into me, our muffs finally meeting for the first time. There are so many sensations at once—a kind of sweet shock that clutches at our vitals—our cunts, nerves, needs. I press back slowly, sliding my hands over your ass to pull you even closer.

"We sway a bit as the water drips from us, slippery and

soaking wet. A sudden breeze wafts in as Bud pulls the shower door open. He's shirtless, his chest heaving with excitement. His hard-on is straining so badly to be freed from his jeans, we can't help but laugh.

"'I need a shower, too, you know,' he says with a pout.

"We part and start to step out of the stall, but you don't let go of my hand. 'Later,' you tell him. 'Don't you want to watch?'"

Doesn't everyone want to watch, Lonely Boy? Racing along the road, I crossed my legs in that lime-green screaming machine. Bud was still surprisingly silent, obviously lost in his own memory of just how lovely—and amazing!—Rita was that day. When she and I spoke about it later on the phone, we both got hot and horny all over again. I asked her to describe to me in detail what had happened between us that afternoon, as if it were happening *at that moment*, and as she did, we both ended up touching ourselves, lustily connecting again, though we were miles apart.

LB, I'm here to tell you that, unlike other types of climaxes, orgasms don't depend on proximity.

No need to share that with Bud—it'll be our secret. You, me, and my old friend Rita. She went on:

"When you ask him if he wants to watch us make love after we step out of the shower, Bud's eyes, already so much like those of a little boy, widen in rapt wonder. You reach for towels, and we dry each other off before you take my hand in yours again. Bud is standing there, seemingly unable to move. Yet he follows us to the bedroom like an obedient little pet. You tell him to go to the chaise and watch us. He groans like a good little creature and sits. Your hand is wrapped around mine as you lead me over to the bed. The knowledge that you are completely into this, our moment together, rushes through me in thrilling waves—and, I confess, with some trepidation. More than anything, I want to please you.

"There are so many ways to touch you. At the bedside, I push you gently so that you now sit. Your towel falls away and you let it, your legs partly open, your breasts gloriously free. I lean over you and trace one hand around the edge of your jaw, my lips close enough to kiss you. But I don't. I want to breathe you in and feel your creamy flesh respond to my touch, to *me*. My fingers patter softly along your neck and shoulders. I lean closer, brushing my cheek against yours, which makes you sigh. Good—that's what I want. I lower my head and start to kiss your neck, eliciting another sigh. Perfect—sing me a song of sighs. My lips wander along the slight dip of your shoulder and lick lightly, my fingers still tracing the edges of you as if you are a fragile, tender map. You moan. I can't help it—I have to kiss you now. I want that moan in my mouth. I want to take you into me.

"You freeze as my lips find yours. Could there be a softer experience in this world? The lushness of our lips meeting, like moist, pulsing pillows. I press my mouth upon yours as gently as a feather might land on a cloud. I brush my top lip across the bottom of yours, painting you with my desire. My fingers dance down your naked arms, pirouetting here, twirling there. You reach out and grab my shoulders, almost as if you're losing your balance.

"That's right, my loveliness. As you relinquish control, passion soars through me. 'What . . . do . . . you . . . want?' I whisper between kisses.

" 'I want you . . . to take me,' you whisper back. 'Please.'

"Of course, my darling. That's exactly what I want, too. I caress your face and hair. I kiss you slowly as I reach down and part your legs with both hands, my tongue softly meeting the sleek velvet of yours and sucking it lightly. That makes you moan again and I pull the sound into me, between my lips, drinking it in, filling me. With my hands meeting around your neck, I grab you closer and ride your lips and tongue with mine.

"Finally, I draw my kiss away and crouch between your legs. You gasp. Yes, my beauty—it's your breasts I want now. I need to tease until you beg me for more. I look over and meet Bud's captivated gaze with a wink. He responds with a big sloppy smile and pops open the button at the waist of his jeans. The sound of a zipper being unzipped follows.

"You are facing him. I turn to watch Bud as his cock springs out—and what a handsome boy it is. No matter what a man looks or seems like, you never know what his prick will be like. In Bud's case, it's quite like him: manly, smooth, yet a little rough around the edges. I imagine that there's a special sensitivity under its ridge, and my appetite whets even more.

"As he lowers his jeans there's a surprise: He shaves his balls. Not something I would have thought, but that's what's so wonderful about human sexuality—there's no telling who will be into what.

"Once he pulls his pants off, he starts to stand up. 'Later,' you say. 'Let me watch you jerk off first.'

"'Aw, baby . . .' he says, but he sits down again, his hard dick in his right hand. 'But since the view's so good . . .' he goes on. You and he smile at each other as I drop my towel and turn back to you, nude and on my knees now. My hands trailing over your nakedness as your breasts jut toward me. I touch them lightly, make small circles around the handfuls, feel in myself the very tingle you must be feeling as you inhale sharply.

"My muff throbs as I lick the middle finger of each hand and slowly daub your nipples. I hear Bud groan behind me, and feel my pussy walls clench in anticipation—I want him to fuck me, but only after my tongue is buried in your snatch and you are begging me to let you come.

"I use both hands to hold one of your breasts and approach it with my mouth. You moan anew. Yes, this is how I want you. 'Spread your legs wider for me,' I whisper. You freeze, suddenly shy. I lick your nipple once, twice. I make my tongue hard. It is hot and the muscle is strong. As I flick it over your tit's tip, you forget your legs and they fall open. That's it, beautiful one, part yourself for me. Give me everything so that I can give everything to you, so I can experience what it feels like to be with you after wanting you for so long. I want to watch your juices seeping out, streaming toward me when I finally dip down my head and— literally—drink you in.

"My thirst for you these many years is only deepening as I flick my tongue across your nipple again and again. You begin to squirm as I speed up. Yes, my love, squirm for me and make those sounds that thrum to the very core of me as I tantalize you. As you start to pant, I move to your other breast—poor baby, so ignored until now.

"With both hands I press into the sensitive flesh and start to suck the nipple lightly, running my tongue in lazy circles around your sweet halo. You moan and I suck harder, your hands grabbing my head and pulling me closer. I hear Bud moan behind me and shake my naked ass for him on purpose, letting him know that I have not forgotten about him as I focus on your pleasure.

"As I suck and flick, lick and thrash, your legs part even wider. Your slit is visible, deep pink and glistening, and I cannot wait much longer. I let go of your breasts, push them together with both hands, and then dart my tongue between them, letting my saliva make them as slippery as I can so that my tongue can skate back and forth with ease.

"You're starting to tremble, and I release your breasts softly, watching them dangle and sway as my mouth rides down your luscious belly, reaching around you to pull you to the edge of the bed so that I might use your legs to help me balance. My lips land on the supple flesh of your inner thigh. That sensitive spot where the leg meets the hip is where my tongue touches first, and you buck at the surprise of it.

"I hear Bud groan behind me, and I use one hand to help push you gently back, so that you can lie comfortably, utterly relax, and then surrender all of yourself to me as I plunder you with my tongue.

"Your sweet legs dangle over the bedside as I kiss your inner thighs. I trail my fingertips over the sleek outside edges of your legs, knowing just what a turn-on that is. As slow as I can make myself tease you, my fingers and my mouth meet at the sexy 'V' where I am about to descend into your dripping bowl of desire.

"You moan, you feel my breath right there, sweeping warmly up and down the lips of your labia. You're so wet, it's hard not to dive in, but I've waited too long for this moment. As lightly as I can, I dip my fingers into your pool and spread your lips so that I can see all of you—your gushing hole, the smooth wall of your perineum, your tight little anus, and the spot that has me mesmerized, your swollen, wanting clit peeking out from under its enticing little hood.

"How much longer can I wait before I wrap my lips around

that precious hood and meet your bursting pearl with the tip of my tongue? First I trail my tongue from the slippery, sensitive spot just below your pussy up into your sopping well. You moan. Yes, my darling, here I am, fucking you with my tongue, entering you as I have always dreamed.

"I hold you there as you start to writhe, one hand on each leg. After I tongue-fuck you for a minute more, I slowly lick up your gash to your clit. I breathe a few breaths as you moan, the hot breeze of me tormenting you. Finally my mouth meets you there and I encircle your clit with my lips. A much deeper groan escapes you. I am here, and here is where I will stay. On my knees, I shake my ass again for Bud—it's an invitation he understands.

"'Room for me?' he asks. I shake my ass again. I know that I am dripping with lust, and I want to be stuffed, pumped, pounded. That's right, gorgeous one, I want your man taking me while I take you, a sweet, tasty sandwich so delicious I will always remember it. And, I promise you, I will eat you so superbly *you* will never forget it.

"In an instant, Bud is behind me, lightly brushing the tip of his stiff prick up and down my sodden, aching slash. 'Mmmmm,' I murmur, my lips over your tender hood, my moan vibrating through my tongue directly to your clit. It makes you writhe, and that is exactly what I want. I lap at you slowly, circling your clit with the edge of my tongue, then stabbing it lightly before riding it flat, drinking in your sighs as your pleasure deepens.

"We become a chain of desire—my hands on your hips, Bud's hands gripping mine as he pushes into me slowly. I moan as you lift your hands to your breasts and start to play with your nipples. Bud kneels behind me and rocks himself back and forth inside me, understanding just how essential it is that he does not pump me too hard right now, not with my tongue tantalizing you as it is. The pounding can wait. I can wait, but not for you. I am not leaving this spot until I make you tremble and cry from the absolute abandon of an unforgettable climax.

"Still circling your clit with my tongue, I pause, starting to suck it lightly between my lips. You gasp and begin to buck, but I hold you down, pulling my mouth away completely. 'No!' you cry, 'Please don't stop! Don't stop!'

"Thank you, my beloved, that is precisely what I want to hear. I lift my head as you lift yours and I look into your eyes. 'I will never stop,' I say. Bud grunts with pleasure and takes this opportunity to pull me back against him. 'Mmmm,' I moan. It's his turn to hold me in place as his thrusts pick up speed and you reach down to hold my hands—we are all still connected.

"Oh, I am reveling in these sensations: how he's plunging into my steamy snatch, how your face reveals your complete abandon, how your pussy lies swollen and waiting for me. I dip into it again and with a groan, Bud slows down. Such a good boy. I need to see you come soon. I've been waiting for this moment for so many years, it's hard to believe it's real.

"But there's your steamy gash, and my tongue is back inside you, pumping you as Bud pumps me. You are panting now and I spread you again with my fingers as my mouth glides back to your clit. I breathe on it once, twice, three times—a breath for each of us—and then curl my tongue and draw a lazy circle around your clitoris that makes you tremble.

"That's right, baby girl, how I love to see you like this, writhing, moaning, squirming, begging me, 'Please!' because that is precisely the point—I exist at this moment to please you. Feel my desire with each flick of my tongue, allow yourself to experience total rapture as I lift my hands to your breasts and gently tug your nips. You start to shiver now, and I know that this is the instant you've crossed the threshold from which is there is no return. From now on, there's only ecstasy.

"My fingers pluck your nipples as if they are the supple strings of a musical instrument, my touch moving in time with my tongue as it circles your clit. Yes, you are like a symphony made flesh as the climax rises from deep inside you, lifting you as you arch your back and bend so beautifully it makes me groan. I lap faster, slower, gently as your cries cut into the air, explosions of bliss, Bud grunting behind me, inside me, as he joins you in this inimitable place, a fucking erotic heaven."

Isn't life absolutely wild sometimes, Lonely Boy?

I shook my head to clear it. The Mustang charged along the road. There were no other cars in sight, the night surrounding us like a big black blanket.

"Oh, baby," Bud said, finally breaking our silence in the car. "You were so damn hot with Rita, beyond hot! Hot as a motherfucker! What I'm trying to say is, baby, you're the best."

I took out my mirror and began to touch up my makeup. Not one syllable would escape these lips.

"What happened tonight is just a bump, a temporary detour on the road to the rest of our lives together. How else are you gonna be the mother of my children?"

That deserved a withering look, and he got one.

He sighed. "Speaking of your mother, I don't know if she had a chance to tell you, but I even called her yesterday to express my sympathy over those hot flashes you told me she was having. I told her I hope she gets well soon, not to worry about that affair your father's having with that fifteen-year-old girl. I said to her, 'Keep your chin up, Mom. Hang tough.'"

What? My father was having an affair with a fifteen year old? Bud actually spilled this to my mother? If it were true, I'm sure my mother had lost it on my father: or had lost it, period. No wonder I hadn't heard from her. I reached into my purse for pen and paper. I made a note to talk to the counselor about possible sedatives for her.

"And by the way, I never said it was okay for him to use my apartment. See? I'm as sensitive as the next guy. And caring and loving and sensitive. SENS-I-TIVE. You write everything down, write that down, SENS-I-TIVE. That's right. I'm not afraid to show my emotions. Write that down, too!"

I folded the piece of paper and stashed it in my bag. For a few blissful moments, Bud was silent. Then:

"Talk to me, baby. C'mon, please . . . Say something! Talk to me, c'mon. . . ."

The road narrowed. Ahead of us, one of those eighteen-wheelers was barreling along.

"You got to . . ."

Bud wet two fingers and ran them over his wounded lip.

"'Cause if you don't, I'm gonna lose touch with my rational self. C'mon, remember that other little person that lives inside of me? Huh? I only had three beers. We're talkin' low blood sugar, we're talkin' . . ."

Bud had sped up again. We were gaining on the truck.

". . . animal instincts . . ."

That was a good way to put it. Bud was overflowing with animal instincts.

"We're talkin' the . . . the world of the criminally insane! Jesus! Mary, mother of God! Talk to me!"

And so religious, too. The truck was right in front of us.

"You know, I was under the impression that our relationship had reached maturity, but I guess I was wrong!"

Maturity? That would mean he had an IQ that had risen into the double digits. We were soaring along the road. Bud gunned it and sailed alongside the truck.

"Talk to me, honey. C'mon, talk to me. Please . . . Say somethin'. Say anythin'."

I looked at him without expression. The 351 swerved toward the truck.

"You really got me goin' now!" he shouted. "There's no turning back. So . . . talk . . . or die! Those are the new rules."

At full speed, the car drove closer to the truck. The truck blew its horn.

"It's your choice," Bud spat out. "You choose. Talk or die!"

Oh no, not this tired old road again. I reached into my bag and pulled out my perfume. I sprayed some onto my décolleté and gently ran my fingers over it. Bud watched, his eyes wide.

"You wanna play rough. Right, you wanna play tough."

He veered toward the truck again. The truck honked again.

"What you don't understand is that I'm bringing stability into your life. That's right. We're in it together."

We raced along the road.

"Live together. Play together. Die together."

This time, he sideswiped the truck. Sparks flew outside my window as the car bounced away and swerved. The truck driver bore down on his horn.

I yawned.

"Talk or die!"

He gunned it and we raced ahead of the truck, cutting it off. I looked back to see that the truck driver had lost control and jackknifed in the middle of the road.

Bud sighed in despair.

"All right," he said. "You win. I give up. I'm a beaten man. Listen, I know what you need. This will calm you down. It's time for our song."

He popped the CD into the player. I rolled down my window, ejected the CD, and tossed it out into the night.

(Good guess, LB—it *was* the Portuguese CD.)

Bud groaned. "Oh God, that's the fifteenth time you've trashed that CD. Isn't there anything that's sacred anymore? Huh?"

He looked at me with bright eyes.

"You know," he started, "all I wanted tonight was to be held. That's it. To be held. Feel protected. Believe me, baby, at times like this I think about growing old all alone. I think back on all those silly mistakes I made, even back there tonight. Thinking back on how different my life could have been if only I'd taken advantage of this opportunity or that."

He looked at me again, his eyes full of sadness.

"Even people with worse luck than me, yeah, I bet if they look back on their lives there was at least one or two opportunities they could have grabbed onto along the way that would've turned everything around. Call it destiny. Call it anything you want. But hooking up with you was the greatest thing in my life. So naturally, what do I do? I set out to destroy it. Why? I don't know why. Because . . . I guess deep down inside I . . . feel like I don't deserve you. . . ."

He paused. Wow, perhaps therapy was actually having an effect.

"I don't know . . . Maybe I'm afraid you'll leave me. All I know is that I couldn't stand to lose you. Because what you are is the golden ring. You're the best thing that's ever happened to me. Like I said, without you I'm just another mechanic on the verge of extinction. But with you there's hope. Blue skies. The way you smell . . . the baby powder you use . . . your perfume. The way you're always somehow wet when I slide my hand down between your legs. With you I get this vision of who I can become instead of who I am. That's the way I feel. But you know, even with all those good things considered, unless you talk to me, unless you open your goddamn mouth and speak in the next fifteen seconds, I'm gonna drive this car through that barricade up ahead. That's right, I mean it, it all comes down to that. Talk or die!"

He hit the accelerator. The car flew.

Fifteen seconds? Not one sound out of me.

"Fifteen . . . fourteen . . ."

Bud's eyes filled with tears and his voice broke.

"You know, even after everything you put me through, I'm here to tell you that nothing else in the whole world means anything to me, but you . . . Seven . . ."

Finally, the speedometer zipped past ninety.

"Six . . . That's right. Because if you don't have love, what's the use in living? Three . . ."

One-hundred-twenty miles an hour!

"Two . . . Talk to me, baby!"

Not a chance. My eyes went blurry with tears.

"One . . . I love you!"

I turned to Bud. He grabbed me as the car hurtled through the fence and plowed through a pile of road barriers. It spun around several times as he tried to regain control of the wheel. We skidded across the concrete and slammed into a cement barrier. Bud yanked the wheel hard and we bounced away, slowing down enough so that when we slammed straight into another barrier, it only ripped through the hood to the engine. Car parts and debris flew through the air.

I landed on top of Bud. His eyes were shut. I started to kiss his face tenderly, praying that he was okay. His eyes slowly opened and he started to say something, but I pressed a finger to his lips, silencing him.

"Shhhhh," I whispered. "I just love foreplay. . . ."

I kissed him full and deep.

Lonely Boy, now you understand. That was always the way he could get me off—with a car. Just seeing that lime-green fucking amazing machine pull into my driveway would make me wet. That big boat of a red Cadillac would beep my horn every time I even *thought* of it. My eyes filled with tears thinking about just how much I'd miss that 351.

One final thought—maybe you should invest in a new car . . . *vroom vroom vroom.*

JAKE

Well, Stella, that's quite an interesting relationship. Some leash she's got on him, eh? A subject you know something about. Talk about compatibility. But I guess it's all about how it looks from the outside. If it fits, it fits. Can you see them when they're about seventy-five years old? She's still setting him up and he's still taking the bait? Just another Saturday night.

As for me, you think I should investigate a new set of wheels? Talk to me, Stella.

Sex in the Hamptons

◆

The Writers' Confessions

ELISE

I'd never known Stacey when her heart had been smashed and pummeled. Her current state was best described as a cross between the music of Metallica and Sarah McLachlan—at least, it was their CDs she'd been blasting. Pointing the remote in her hand like a gun, she bulleted between the two very distinct moods as she recounted her experience with the Italian Bastard.

My head jerked this way and that between the cascading, melodious ache of Sarah and the explosive rage of the black leather-clad screaming men. Stacey was determined to board a flight for Italy the next day, and I had to use every therapeutic trick I could muster to keep her stateside.

If provoked, a Double Scorpio was capable of violence. Not that we all weren't, but Stingers possessed a ferocious belief that violence *is* the answer, not just a fantasy or a last resort. She truly wanted to murder Jocko.

When she flipped to Sarah, I aligned myself with Stacey's fragile, weeping heart. I used words to soothe: "Poor baby." "Oh, sweetie." "I'm so sorry." She soaked up the tenderness, but only for so long and then *WHACK!* The percussive slaying rage of Metallica returned, shattering my tender tones—and my eardrums.

And yet, at my friend's side, I had to rage, rage at the dying of the Italian. "He should be shot," I said. "Tortured. Stabbed in the heart. Ripped asunder by a pack of wolves."

Stacey paced, scheming and plotting Jocko's demise. Her well-muscled arms tightened, her fists clenched, her jaw clamped. She was a seasoned writer and had ghosted in the past on best-selling crime novels, those really exacting whodunits that left you guessing until the last chapter ended. I believed Stacey could actually pull off whatever she was mentally concocting, and my job was to stop her.

After two hours of emotional whiplash, I suggested a walk, and convinced her that even if the travel agent called back, we could still make the rest of her arrangements online, even book a hotel room and rent a gondola, if she wanted. She already had her e-ticket printed.

We strolled along her bay beach at Lazy Point, and I remarked that I understood why this was one of her favorite places in the world, a particular spot where two tides met and mingled.

"Who cares?" she snarled. "There's no fucking beauty in this world."

Our shoes crunched over shells and stones perfect for skipping. I had to resist bending to pick up one of these flat round wonders to launch, fearing the action would anger Stacey. Right now it was her heart that had been flung across the water, bouncing and careening and sinking in the depths of her being.

"Y'know, Stace, the most potent weapon you have is words. Writing is the best revenge."

Her eyebrows vaulted. "Hmm," she responded.

I continued: "What about doing a story for the fiction section of the *East Hampton Star*? They love your stuff. It'll be about a famous Italian sculptor named Jocamo who creates enormous figures of naked women to compensate for his impotence and repressed homosexual impulses."

A slight smirk crossed her face as she listened.

"Murder him on the page, baby," I pressed. "Write a scene where he throws a lavish Hamptons' party, and all the servers are gorgeous, young gay men he tries to seduce."

"That's it!" she declared. "And the women he sculpts are all references to the sick, incestuous relationship he had with his beloved, devouring, Italian mother."

"Don't forget that spaghetti is straight before you cook it," I added.

"And I'm gonna boil his penne ass," she sneered.

"That's my writing partner."

I picked up an ideal stone, and I was about to calculate its release when Stacey interrupted.

"We could also break into his house and trash it," she said.

I sighed. "Trash his reputation," I answered. "Let's stay out of the crime blotter in *Dan's Papers*. We're about to land a book deal, remember?"

"We won't get caught," she insisted. "I know where the key is."

"Stacey, call me crazy, but I don't think there's a market for newly discovered children's book authors who live behind bars."

I finally let the stone sail, and the first bounce on the surface of the water sent it high, "getting good air," as a skateboarder would say. The second, third . . . and then eighth meeting of stone on its liquid sky was, quite frankly, astonishing.

Of course, Joe would have been impressed, but since our last romp I hadn't heard from him and I didn't think I would. I believed we were finished, but in a good way. We had spent ourselves and freed each other in one long, luxurious sexual weekend of raw, uncommitted, unreserved, sweaty, full-on fucking. I hadn't longed to hear from him, in fact. I believed we had written and completed the perfect ending to our affair.

I picked up one last stone, almost as a ritual farewell to Joe. As the stone skimmed across the water's surface, time seemed to stop as our last wild excursion played through my mind like a beloved film:

He pulled me hard against him, his arms winding around my back, his hands, insatiable, exploring, as his opened mouth found mine. His hot tongue filled me, sucking with such intensity my knees went weak. He groaned, his hands holding my ass cheeks, pressing me into his simmering, hardening groin. My cunt was churning, roaring, ocean-wet, desire spilling out of me in wave upon wave. That delirious sensation of raw, physical need flowed through my body. Urgent. Vital.

My own hands greeted his newly muscled back, felt the flexibility and strength, the warm heat of his flesh under his sweater. My fingers celebrated the lack of softness, the brick solidity of Joe—a man, thank God, a man! It had been too long.

Still encased in his jeans, his escalating, hard-as-concrete cock seemed to complete the space between my legs as he lifted me easily, rocking my hips against his scorching crotch of explosive need. My clit ballooned against my own jeans. I wasn't wearing panties, and I could feel my clit ignite in a wet blaze as Joe kept rocking me against him. Our tongues were indiscernible—melted, fused together. Low, belly-deep moans from both of us filled the air.

Time didn't exist. It stretched and extended beyond seconds, minutes, hours. How I missed this girth, the rough stubble of his cheek against mine, the raw power of his limbs. He could overcome me, force me, fuck me with the sheer strength of his body com-

pared to mine. This dominance ushered within me a kind of sweet submission. I welcomed it.

Stacey's voice broke my reverie: "You had twelve fucking bounces, bitch. Damn, I'm impressed."

I knew Joe would have smiled. *Bye, Joe.*

STACEY

She can be very persuasive, my writing partner. It took a while to convince me, but perhaps because of her background as a former clinical psychologist, her skills finally soared over the impenetrable wall otherwise known as my stubborn, rebellious nature. It was really the question of whether or not I wanted to spend the rest of my life in prison and have my sex life reduced to my booty being plugged by a broom handle or another obviously mundane item by ten, twelve, or even hundreds of ugly, dangerously criminal chicks. That thought made me realize that murdering Jocko was just not worth it.

Not even close, given my resistance to authority as well. Think of the possibly equally ugly, obviously sadistic prison guards telling me what to do, and this little girl actually having to do whatever it was they wanted, or off to solitary confinement I'd go. I mean, much as I adore being alone at times, enforced confinement is not freedom (being on deadline, of course, is quite similar. . . . Still, I get to pace back and forth, drink vast quantities of tea and other intoxicants, and ponder the destiny of the deer in the backyard.) As for prison, I'm not necessarily thinking of rape and pillage, either. Those corrections officers might even order me to cook!

Besides, it was October, and early fall in the Hamptons was too spectacularly gorgeous to miss. There was the heart-pounding hurricane surf, the trees slowly blanketed by the changing colors of their leaves before they wafted to the ground in bright piles, the uncrowded eateries and emptying roads, and—you've already guessed what I'm about to say—the blissful wind.

Recently, one early evening, when the breeze picked up and started whipping around the sky, I took a drive out to Montauk with all the car windows down, the CD player blaring that remarkable tune from Evanescence, "Bring Me to Life."

Indeed.

As I gunned the gas pedal and shifted into fifth gear while heading east, I shouted out the lyrics alongside those two phenomenal singers. While the words moved through me and the wind whooshed in and out of the car, another part of myself vowed that in no way would I allow my former dark-haired dream of Italianitude ruin my certifiable zeal for passion.

Let us not forget that the Double Scorpio in question actually had Scorpio in *four* places in her chart, which meant that I was even more prone to waltzing through the dance between life and death, possessed by a vast capacity to resurrect, and that Immortality might just as well be my middle name.

(Don't bother asking the real one, my brilliant scribe. Certain ridiculous realities are just never going to leave these lips, so please lose the curiosity and replace it with my gratitude.)

ELISE

You know when a quality in a person you care for is endearing and annoying at the same time? (Close your eyes, Writing Partner, this is about you.)

Let me digress for a moment. I called our mutual friend, Annie, a gorgeous guru of spiritual wisdom and shopping precision—essentials for a full life.

I left her a message: "Annie, Elise. Stacey. Heartbroken. Shopping. Stat."

Within five minutes Annie called back: "Twenty minutes. Henry Lehr."

We were dedicated to finding the most superlative, sexiest outfit imaginable for Stacey's recovery. Within forty-five minutes, Annie had worked her genius, transforming our double Scorp into a sexy vision in black and white.

Stepping out of the dressing room wearing tight, white jeans and a top that clung to her as if it were her own skin, Stacey's hands caressed her indomitable thighs: "They're like butter," she exclaimed. "God, I'd give anything to touch myself."

Restoration complete.

The three of us ambled along Newtown Lane in East Hampton. With shopping bags in tow, Stacey stepped ahead of us as we entered Citta Nuova for a late lunch. I noticed her former confident, slightly cocky swagger begin to return.

As we were seated, she said: "Did you see those guys at the bar? They were staring at my breasts."

Endearing and annoying. Why? *We* had breasts, too. And might I add—though I would never let Stacey know this—that if I were a man (or woman for that matter) *my* eyes would have been fixed on *Annie's* heavenly legs.

Of course, the waitress was Stacey's next target. "She is *so* flirting with me," she whispered. "Did you notice how she grazed my hand with hers when she took my menu?"

Annie and I nodded in unison, kicking each other under the table, allowing our shipwrecked friend her need to be desired by absolutely everyone. Endearing because, yes, it makes up for the empty parts. Annoying because, in those moments, my Scorpio friend forgets that the Annies and the Gupsters of this world are also coveted by many.

However, I have one caveat. Stacey's Scorpio-squaredness caused her to emit a sensual, seductive vibration that often made male dogs in heat—especially German shepherds—chase her car when she passed. I had witnessed this phenomenon, no lie.

So swagger forth, Writing Partner, and flourish.

STACEY

"Bring Me to Life." You can say that again. Without question, it was time to expand my territory. As the song ended, I wondered how far I would go. And what would life be like with my heart out of the picture? It was not as if my favorite little muscle had gone on vacation; rather it had burst into countless sharp splinters of disappointment, incredulity, and despair after Mr. Amazing Hands had finally unveiled the truth and said that he was leaving for Venice the next morning to see his family. Until that moment, I'd had no inkling that there was a WIFE, to say nothing of SONS and DAUGHTERS, too.

And even though I'd ripped up my e-ticket—along with what was left of my naiveté—and tossed the remnants of it into the trash can with Elise as my witness (at her insistence, but you already know that), I still fantasized about what I would do were I ever to arrive in that unfamiliar world of gondolas and ageless canals. Maybe seduce his wife over wine and delectable cheeses? Given my history as a straight chick, that didn't seem likely—although I do love cheese.

Well, what about his sons? How much would it bother Jocko if I fucked each and every one of them? Nah. In a strange way, that would just make me even closer to him. Maybe snare one into proposing marriage and then leave him in the lagoon? Not fair—I did not want to hurt someone *else*, only Jacopo Bellini himself.

Perhaps something more like hiring a *pulcino* to seduce him and then have his wife show up unexpectedly? But that would hurt *her*—again not my intention. And maybe she already knew he fooled around on her and didn't even care. In that case, my attempt would fall pretty flat. And how could that even be, given his wicked skill as a world-class seducer and lover. The bastard fuckhead.

(Help me out here at any time, Writer Pal. You Double Pisces any good at revenge? I'm going to lean to the left of that one, meaning "no" but, of course, feel free to contradict.)

More realistically, his house and studio nestled on my side of the world might be where I went next. It was entirely possible that a raging fire might roar through them some mysterious, windy night. Because art was so important to me, though, I think I'd have to spare the studio. Besides, that space, teeming with chicks of all shapes and sizes, sculpted from iron, steel, wood, stone, a collection of brows, chins, torsos, breasts, backs of knees, and eyelids, now housed a pile of some pretty incredible memories of mine. To say nothing of the resonant echoes of my ecstatic cries when I climaxed there, especially the very first time Mr. Dark Eyes had draped me over that brilliant, enormous white marble buttock and catapulted me into an entirely new reality. And by this I mean plunging into my back door with one magnificent stroke, only after I'd soared beyond heaven, surrendering to the rhapsodic way he had ridden my clit and streaming gash as if he himself were the big man upstairs.

Damn, revenge was a complicated beast. I'd keep plotting. After all, revision was everything in writing. (Additional suggestions, Guppy Girl?)

Meantime, I had just crested the hill and begun my descent into Montauk, the sea shimmering like a rippling vision, the setting sun behind me casting a golden glow across the water. Talk about evanescent!

As if with a mind of its own, my car turned left onto Second House Road, and I headed the back way, hugging one edge of Montauk's many ponds as I approached the harbor. A few minutes later, I rolled into the parking lot of Dave's Grill. Yes, exactly, the scene of the seduction, the beginning of the end, the very spot where Mr. Dark and Sultry and I had met for the first time. Apparently, I could not stop myself.

Was this the way to heal? (Ms. Clinical Psych, get back to me on this, please. After all, it's been said that novelists are very similar to psychologists. We just come to it naturally, without the training, so I would appreciate the feedback. As you know, I almost always go with my gut, and in this case, with my car driving my snatch—oops, I mean leading the way—who knows what impulse I was really following.)

Life, of course, would have me find out. I greeted Brian, the bartender, and sat down on the corner stool at one end of the U-shaped bar, my favorite place to perch and watch the world. After a bit of innocent chitchat (I hadn't seen him since meeting Mr. Long Eyelashes, of course), Brian landed me with a double *Porfidio blanco*, a lustrous glass of tequila.

One, two sips. I looked around. The usual batch of Hamptonites—moneyed, seemingly important, decidedly self-important, poised to demand that you get out of their way, were they in search of the perfect tomato or ear of corn, because, as you know, their next meal is the utmost important thing in the world.

Yet next to me, another kind of couple sat with their backs to the crowd. He was a big-boned, thirty-something guy with tousled black hair and feral, sexy eyes, seated next to what appeared to be his wife, given the simple gold rings each wore. She had baby-fine locks the color of narcissus that fell just past her shoulders and contrasted nicely with the sharp features of her face. Her eyes were almond shaped and intensely curious, darting about as she took in the activity around her.

Contrary to the more popular, local custom that dripped Major Attitude, she sailed a sweet smile my way as our eyes met, then the man turned toward me.

"These are good nuts," he said, referring to the bowls of peanuts on the bar.

"Glad to hear it," I said, noticing that he was downing an imported beer, and his wife, a glass of red wine. "Nothing like a good nut."

He looked at me full-on and then laughed.

I smiled back.

"You live out here?" he asked.

"I do. Guess you don't?"

"Up-island. Out for a long weekend."

The wife was still smiling at me.

"Lucky you," she said. "It's so beautiful out here."

"I know. Every season, too," I said. "Where are you guys staying?"

"Gansett Green Manor, in Amagansett," he said.

"You know the place?" she asked.

"Sure. I know the owner—interesting dude. I like the sculpture on the front lawn." Though the thought had just burbled out, the word "sculpture" clawed through me.

"Sculpture?" he asked.

"Oh, right. You know, honey," she went on, "out front. It's like a bed of nails, but with individual rocks on top of each rod." She laughed, looking at me. "That's not a very good description."

"Actually, I think it is," I managed. "Up close it's funkier than that, though. Since the rods are all different sizes."

My gaze drifted across the bar to the spot where I had first seen Mr. Bullet Butt. Doomed, I remembered *his* rod instantly.

"I've always been curious about a single woman watching a couple in public," the guy next to me said, those intense eyes digging into me. "Is she content to watch or does she do something bold?"

"WHAT?" I sputtered, grateful that he had made me stop thinking, for the moment, of Jocko.

"Richard!" His wife elbowed him.

I burst out laughing. "You've got balls. . . ."

His wife laughed, too. "Yah, on the brain. So sorry."

"I don't mind," I said.

"I figured that," he offered.

"That right?" I asked. "How many beers have you had?"

He laughed. "Not enough. You just look like a girl who knows what's what."

"Woman, honey. She looks like a *woman*. . . ."

"You're telling me," Richard added.

He grinned at me as Brian made his way to our end of the bar.

"Can we buy you a drink?" The wife offered.

"Uh, sure," I said.

"I'm Maria," she said.

"Stacey," I replied.

"Richard," he added.

"As we know," I answered.

"So what do you do, Stacey?" Richard asked.

"I'm a writer."

"Really? And you make a living doing that?"

Again, Maria elbowed him. "Richard . . ."

"Not a problem," I said. "Actually, one of the projects I'm working on right now is an erotic fiction series."

"Get out!" he blurted. "That is smoking hot!"

"That's exactly right," I answered.

Maria blushed a bit as Brian brought our drinks. I lifted mine and said, "Cheers."

"*Salut!*" Richard beamed. "Here's to you!"

"Cheers," Maria offered a bit shyly, but the look in her eyes was the opposite of bashful.

That was the moment I thought this pair might be a bit more than your usual, average couple from up-island.

"So what's a beautiful girl like you doing alone on a Sunday night?" he queried. A waitress came and delivered their food—mussels and lobsters.

I smiled. "You're sweet. The wind made me do it. I'm taking a break from my deadlines."

"Are you single?" Maria asked. Again her voice was timid, but the boldness of her gaze was the opposite.

"Yeah," I said. "I prefer it that way."

"Tell me more," she said. Was that seductive?

Richard leaned in closer. This was getting more interesting.

"I like my freedom," I explained. "That way, I can do what-ever I want. . . . If you get my drift."

"Mmmm," Richard said.

Maria smiled and nodded. I noticed that we were all drinking our cocktails at championship speed. Richard motioned to Brian for another round.

"Would you like to join us for dinner?" Maria asked. "Please, help yourself to the mussels."

"Uh, thanks," I said. "They do a great calamari here."

After I'd ordered, Richard asked, "So do you have any experience with the kind of scenario I asked you about before?"

"You mean with a couple?" I answered.

"Mmm hmm," he said.

Maria was alternately blushing and smiling. Was this turning her on or was she merely buzzed?

"Well," I replied, "I wrote a story about a woman getting on a train in Paris routed to Nice. A strange man winks at her as she walks through the train compartment on the way to the bar car. On her way back, she loses her balance. He leaps up, and squeezes her hand. She lets him. Without a word, he leads her back through the cars to the end, where a woman is sitting alone in that compartment. The woman acts like she's completely oblivious to their presence as the guy starts to make love to my girl. Remember, not a word spoken."

"Really?" Maria chirped. "That's wild!"

I laughed, pleased at her slow bloom.

"So what happens next?" Richard blurted.

I patted him on the forearm. "Down, boy. What happens is that you'll have to buy the book to find out."

He groaned with true misery.

"My, my," Maria said. "You are something of a tease, aren't you?"

"I do my best," I replied.

We laughed.

"You're a trip," Richard said. "We will definitely buy your book."

"Great. That's at least one sale made on Long Island."

"So is it the type of story we'd want to read to each other?" Maria asked.

"No question. You'll be at it for days."

Richard guffawed. "Honey, you're the one with the balls!"

I smiled at him. "No question about that, either."

(Yes, Elisimo, I hear you—it's a bit much, but as we know I like to toss in a little grandiosity to make up for the empty parts. In this particular instance, that would be the small yet sprawling space vacated by my once intact and thriving heart.)

Maria was blushing again. "So, Stacey, are you the type of girl who would go for a train ride like the one you wrote about?"

"Hmm, that's a good question. Don't forget there were *two* women—the one who participated and the one who watched."

She grinned. "Oh, right. So which one would you be?"

"Which one would *you* be?" I replied.

Maria was obviously a master blusher. "I asked you first."

"And two is more than one. I asked second."

Richard laughed. "Now, now, girls. Let's play nice."

Maria smacked him in the arm. "I think I would like to watch," she admitted.

"And I would definitely like to play," I said, distinctly meeting Richard's gaze.

"Really! God, I love the Hamptons," he beamed. "You like that double-decker the LIRR runs these days?"

"Never been on it," I said. "I spend most of my time at my desk making up stories like the one I just started to tell you."

"Right," Maria said, "the strangers on a train. That sounds familiar. . . ."

"And I quote," I went on, *"Their breath quickened as their tongues tasted each other's, and the man's hardening erection now strained against his trousers. She swayed a bit as his fingers began to play her nipples through her blouse. He knew just how to touch her, it seemed. The pressure he exerted between thumb and index finger so perfectly orchestrated, it was as if he had always known what she wanted and had done just that.'"*

"Shit!" Richard said.

"Shit," Maria echoed.

"That *is* smoking hot," Richard continued.

"And so are you," Maria crooned.

I was not usually a blusher but having a straight girl say that kind of remark soared right through me. Fuck, an echo of Gabrielle, my only dream in that respect.

"Oh! Well, thank you," I said.

My calamari arrived and I began to eat it, savoring the additional hot sauce I always asked for. My unexpected dinner dates feasted on their lobsters.

Between bites, I watched as Maria and Richard glanced at each other in that knowing way that married couples do.

"So, we, I mean, would you . . ." Maria started.

"We mean," Richard blurted, "is it possible that we could all, you know, ever get together?"

"You mean . . ." I took a long breath in. "It might be possible, but never on a first date."

"Pff, well, sure, of course," he blabbered.

"I like to get to know someone a little bit, you know what I mean?" I added. "See how much juice is really there. . . ."

Maria nodded in fast-forward. "I know exactly what you

mean. We're just a normal, married couple. It's not like we do this all the time or anything."

"But you've done it before?" I asked.

She blushed again. "A few times."

"So I guess you had a good time."

The smile on Richard's face was now his most prominent feature. "Ohhh, man, it was fucking smoking hot!"

Maria belted him again. "Enough with the 'smoking hot,' huh!"

"Hmmm," I said.

The restaurant was now cranking at full force. People stood in layers behind us, a little too close for our increasingly intimate chat. We had just finished our meals.

"Listen," I suggested, "you guys want to take a walk out by the dock?"

"Sure!" Maria yelped.

"Great idea," Richard agreed.

I reached into my jeans for some cash, but Richard shooed that idea away with a wave of his hand. I watched as he laid down what was obviously the bill amount plus a hefty tip. Made me want to kiss him. I dug it when people were aware of other people's needs.

I said good night to Brian and we split. Outside, the wind had hushed, the night a cool blanket. It was dark, yet the moon cast enough light to illumine our stroll. We walked toward the harbor, over the worn wooden planks where the boats glided in and dumped the fish they'd caught. The eons of footfalls that had trampled over it were evident from the dock's pocked and pitted surface. I found this oddly soothing. Could have been the tequila talking—we were all pretty tipsy by now.

Richard wrapped his arm around his wife's shoulder. "Maria wants to totally seduce someone. Would you be game?"

"Richard!" Maria said. She bounced against him.

I laughed, as much out of surprise as nerves. "It's okay. To tell you the truth, I've never been with a woman before."

"Get out!" he blurted.

"Really?" Maria asked. "Someone as beautiful as you?"

"You are the sweetest," I said. "But really. I think I was sort of in love with a woman I've known for years but we never made it to bed, and now she's not speaking to me."

"Because you wouldn't do her?" Richard asked.

I looked away. "Fuck. Because I was in love with someone else when she was finally ready. Bad timing."

"So the someone else was a guy?" Maria queried.

"Yeah." I could feel the sorrow welling up from the deepest part of me. *Get out of my mind, Mr. Sultry Lips. You've already ripped my heart into nothing.*

I cleared my throat. "Actually, I met him at the bar we just left."

"Oh!" Richard exclaimed. "So is Dave's like your lucky place?"

I could feel the frown grip my mouth. "I think at this moment my heart would say no."

"Aww, I'm so sorry," Maria offered.

We stood facing each other in one corner, overlooking the bay as it sloshed against the dock. Maria reached over and patted my arm. She was a sweetheart. They both were, actually. There was something so sincere and easy about them.

"Let's change the subject," I suggested. "You guys are a lot of fun."

"No problem," Richard said. "And likewise. Maria takes very little time to come. She can explode for hours—"

"Richard!" Maria protested, wobbly footed as she reared back and then smacked his chest with her hand.

Richard and I both laughed as he grabbed her hand and held her against him. Their passion for each other was evident.

"She wants to totally seduce someone," he repeated. "Would you be game?"

"Uh, I don't know," I answered. That was the truth at the moment, but as I looked at the still-blushing Maria with her bold, unbroken gaze, I felt another truth rising: It was time to shake it up. (Double Gulp: It was just not my style to languish in the dark wake of Betrayal's path. That's right, I had to get it the hell out of my way.) Hearted or heartless, I was determined to experience as much as I could in this life.

"Do you want to give me your number?" I asked. "How long are you guys staying?"

"Just till tomorrow," she peeped.

Richard was already reaching into his wallet for a business card. He handed it to me. "I work at home, so—the obvious."

"I may have to go to the city tomorrow for business," I explained. "After I get back, maybe I'll give you a call later in the week?"

"Sure!" Maria said.

"Great," Richard said.

"Cool," I said.

"In the meantime, I gotta find out what happened to those two on the train," Richard announced.

We all laughed.

"Speaking of work, it's getting late," I said.

"Sure, of course!" Maria said. "Listen, it was really great meeting you. . . ."

"Ditto," Richard offered. He reached out to shake hands.

I grabbed his and pulled him toward me.

"You can do better than that!" I challenged.

He laughed and lobbed one onto my lips. I pulled away and turned to Maria.

"So I guess it's bye for now," I said.

"I guess so," she nearly whispered.

I opened my arms and she stepped toward me. We embraced tentatively as I pressed my cheek against hers.

How sweet was that?

Sweet Maria. Ballsy Richard. What a combo.

ELISE

C was due to return tomorrow, and I longed for her in every sense of the word. Physically. Emotionally. Intellectually. Sexually. I wanted to feel her toes greet mine as we slept, experiencing that greeting as it creeps into my dreams and finds expression in the night world of slumber.

They say familiarity breeds contempt, but the absence of familiarity can give birth to a desire for those things that had become numbing, boring, or even contemptible. After separation, anticipation for what was known seemed to usher in an excitement, as if we were meeting for the first time. Absence and distance should be a requirement in all relationships to stave off the dulling of routine, the overexposure and lack of mystery that constancy often seemed to create.

We'd all seen those couples sitting across from each other in a restaurant with absolutely nothing to say, as if they'd been rendered mute because too many minutes, hours, days, and years together had left them speechless and blind. Nothing left to discover. No more layers to peel back. Surprise had been packed in a box of old photos and forgotten, dusted over and molding in the attic of memories.

That was why I tried not to take my lovers for granted. One moment could change everything: life was that unpredictable, our control over it a phantom we tricked ourselves into believing. Love and desire were ephemeral and unknown, like death. That was exactly why love and lust were not to be wasted or meted out like an allowance to a child. Love should be spent extravagantly, like a winning slot machine exploding with cash. Sex, too, like hitting the jackpot, the billion-dollar Lotto.

We were, after all, creatures created, depending on your beliefs, to fully, wildly, wholly express our humanness. So when I said to Stacey, "Go forth and have great sex," I was telling her the prescription for the moment, a way to cross from one place to another. The truth is, none of us knew very much, but we did our best. We fumbled and stumbled, writhed and rose and constantly wrestled with the insane terrain called love.

STACEY

After I climbed into the car, it continued to have a mind of its own and rolled me away from the harbor and across the breadth of Montauk, toward the ocean. By now it had to be after midnight—I had left my cell phone home. I decided that was beautiful. A stroll by the sea would definitely be a welcome close to this unusual evening.

Outside of the distant stars and the faraway moon, there was no light. The ocean was a crashing, soothing sound that calmed me in the black, inky cocoon I walked through. My only companion was the sand urging my feet forward. Ah, my beloved sea, my forever love.

Somewhere in a nearby beach house, music leaked out, Brazilian dance rhythms along with bursts of booze-induced laughter. In my mind, I could see the party: white folks with deep tans wondering who had the most money and the biggest house, while their monstrous SUVs were protected outside by Hispanic valets probably wondering if this crowd would tip them well or be too drunk to remember that they even existed.

Before me, I spied a flickering light. It looked as though a fire-fly had decided, as I had, to seek the solitude of the beach. As I drew nearer, I smelled the familiar sweet odor of marijuana, and it guided me to the source like a whispered prayer. I calculated that I stood about five feet away,

"Are you sharing?" I called softly.

"Happily," a man's voice replied, although I did not detect any sliver of happiness in it. In fact, I was struck by the incongruous empty aloneness that permeated from the sound of the word he had spoken. In the darkness we were but blurs to each other, the tip of the lit joint illuminating our hands as he offered it to me.

I pulled in a deep drag and realized that the faint glow from the burning bud must have wafted across my face, disappearing just as quickly as I extended the joint to my shadowy stranger.

"From the party?" he asked.

"No," I said.

"Good," he replied. "The whole thing is a waste of oxygen."

"Not exactly in the party mood?"

He didn't answer, but took a long pull off the joint, which enabled me to catch my own firefly glimmer of his face. About thirty, maybe younger, his complexion was unblemished, with soft, sad brown eyes and a sharp dimpled chin. Ah, good genes and moneyed beauty. *Why so cynical, so melancholy,* I wondered? *Heart-smashed like me?*

"I thought you were a firefly when I saw the light from your joint," I said.

"Is that why you came over?" he asked.

"Exactly. Looking for a glowing companion in the dark."

"A woman alone at one in the morning on a dark beach?"

"Ocean therapy," I answered.

"Bad night, Woman Alone?"

"No, not bad, Sad Eyes, just moving through time."

He sighed. It sounded like a gentle, pining breeze that licked through the beach reeds.

"Bad party?" I asked.

"Pitiful."

"So why don't you just leave?"

"My house," he chuckled, resigned. "What should I do?"

"I don't give parties," I said. "And I rarely attend them, so outside of spraying your guests with an AK-47, I have no advice."

We both laughed. The reverberation between us embraced like sea to shore.

"What do you do?" he asked.

"Nothing." The word came out without a thought. "Nothing that matters in this moment, I mean."

"Then we share common ground."

A silent something passed between us as he stubbed out the joint.

"Do you know that song lyric, 'Save me from the nothing I've become'?" I asked.

"No."

"I prefer *celebrate* the nothing I've become."

He laughed again. "Did God send you?"

"You better hope not," I replied.

From his house a shattering crash punctured the air, followed by streams of enervated laughter.

"Shouldn't you check it out?" I asked.

"And leave the only person in the world who makes sense to me?"

For a nanosecond, I hesitated. "No names," I said simply.

"No names," he responded.

I stripped off my black silk shirt. Next, the new, buttery smooth white jeans melted down my legs, and I stepped out of them easily. I was not wearing a bra or panties.

"Give me your hand," I said.

I reached out and found his, our bodies mere silhouettes although we now stood close. I guided his hand to my breast, and he sighed, cupping the right one in his palm.

"A silent stripper," he whispered, as both of his hands explored me, slow, deliberate, absorbing each sinew of my arms, my waist, my ass.

Denied true sight, other senses take over. Our cheeks caressed the other's, breathing in the scent of the jasmine oil I had applied earlier. His smell was dry cedar, rich, heady, nothing false or pretentious.

My tongue licked the crevice on his chin, trailed to his neck, dipped into an ear. We weren't making any sounds, as if we were not only blind but mute as well. I clutched his T-shirt and pulled it up over his head, and then reached down to discover he was wearing cotton drawstring shorts that slipped down his achingly tight body with ease.

When our mouths merged, we shared the taste of the weed. Our tongues and lips were a perfect match, a wordless, soundless dance of anonymous need and desire meeting the dark ocean's resounding collision with the shore.

Our hands read each other like Braille, fingers inching across flesh, my slice throbbing as our torsos and hips met for the first time. His hardening cock felt warm, long, and desperate, but in a way that made me want to take him in my mouth and offer everything and take everything, while both of us continued to be nothing.

I dropped to the sand, my knees sinking into the gravely bed as my hands clenched his ass cheeks and my mouth, open and hungry, found his cock—ready, thickening, and even longer than I had imagined.

The woody scent of his flesh now mingled with a tincture of salt and ripe, tangy sweat. In this moment our voices returned with twin groans of pleasure and relief, as if for both of us a burden had been lifted.

(Yo, Elise—notice the burden being lifted even though my heart was already clearly unburdened as a result of its nonexistence. Interesting paradox, right?)

His hands rested lightly on my head, caressing my hair, not guiding or demanding me to perform in any way. His openness to let the moment of discovery happen was as wide as my mouth undulating against his precious prick.

I draped one arm around his ass to steady him, and with my free hand, I knowingly began to pet and squeeze his thrumming balls. They were decorated with startling soft hairs, like that on a newborn baby.

"Mmmm," I murmured as I played them, feeling the sound I made reverberate against his pulsing shaft. With each breath, Sad Eyes emitted delicate, deep notes of satisfaction. The scent from his damp thatch of hair mixed with the sea salt and my own saliva made me feel giddy and higher than I already was, as if I could have lapped at this place for the rest of my life, and in so doing I would come to realize all that existence on this earth promised.

I wanted to suck and gag, lick and devour his staff, the cock of a strange man on a dark beach with no name and no need to define himself—or me. Instead of reaching for categories of familiarity, we had released ourselves and had surrendered to the exchange of flesh and fluids.

My pussy dripped like a slow faucet, my syrupy juices spotting the sand below me. My tongue thrashed against him and my lips squeezed hard as they rode his rod faster and faster.

Sad Eyes's thighs trembled. As I gently squeezed his balls, he jerked back, then thrusted. His hot semen cascaded down my throat, and I took him in greedily, gulping in as much of his milk as I possibly could.

He dropped to his knees and pushed me onto my back, spreading my legs wide with his hands. As if guided by an invisible honing device, his surprisingly coarse, unsurprisingly long tongue landed on my insanely needy, swelling nub. He was as greedy as me, tasting my wet juices, licking my inner thighs, and sliding his tongue from my clit to my ass with abandon. We were both so thirsty, hungry, and wanting. "Drink, eat, be merry," each crashing wave seemed to say, "for soon the tide may change."

He slowed, sucking my outer lips, one then the other. In between, his tongue titillated my newly awakened pearl.

And it was in that moment that salty tears sprang from my eyes. My cunt was a conch shell roaring with the cry of a hundred oceans, even of seas long ago formed and now extinct.

As if sensing it all, my stranger, my soul-mate-in-the-moment, focused his tongue on releasing my pearl from her shell.

The perfect painting strokes of his wet brush caused a flurry of colors to erupt across the canvas of my closed eyes—cerulean blue, seaweed green, phosphorescent orange, fish-silver flash.

All at once, the plaintive call of a pod of whales echoed through the dark sky, tripping across the sea, causing tides to swell, making waves bloom and froth. A deeper part of me suddenly realized that it was *my* voice bellowing as I climaxed, and a brand new ocean erupted from my eyes and flowed down my cheeks to my breasts where now my sad-eyed man swam like a child. His mouth, his face, his curly head of hair and gorgeous tongue, they dove at my breasts as if they were waves.

I held onto his head as if for precious life.

When I woke, the faintest hint of light daubed the sky. I was wearing his T-shirt and shorts, and my own clothes had been folded neatly and served as a pillow for my head.

He was gone.

I sat up, sand-covered and bleary, gazing at my altar—the Atlantic. My clit pulsed, remembering.

What a fucking amazing night.

Gupster, this one's going to make you wail: Only later when I got home did I find a note tucked into my jeans pocket: *Maybe you were sent by God after all,* he wrote. *I now celebrate the nothing I've become.*

For there within me I felt it: resurrected, recharged, renegotiable.

I finally got around to checking my phone messages. When I pressed the button on the machine it announced: "You have eleven new messages." Huh? Had Jocko had a change of heart?

I grabbed my cell: It displayed that I had ten new messages. I listened to my machine first.

Twenty-one out of twenty-one? Who would have bet the odds on that? At the moment, it was all *good* news.

ELISE

My long anticipated reunion with C was delayed for another night. There was only one thing that could have impelled me to leave the very day of her arrival home: a significant six-figure offer from a publisher and a dinner celebration with our beloved agent, W. D., along with a night at the Four Seasons.

We were doing back flips, Stacey and I, barely able to contain our outrageous delight from everyone we encountered.

As it turned out, our "Lame Duck" children's book series had found a hot editor and a very enthusiastic sales force at Penguin Group. Now, the first *Lame Duck Goes to Peking* title was scheduled for a fast-track release next spring. We were going to quack and waddle all the way to the bank.

On the Jitney ride into the city (the Ambassador bus, mind you. It cost more money, but offered that extra legroom and wine gratis), we recounted our fantasies about W. D. I had only recently met her. Stacey, of course, had known her for several years.

We'd had lunch at Mix where they served peanut-butter-and-jelly appetizers, among other more sophisticated fare. Unfortunately, after lunch, W. D. was running late to her next appointment and meted out too quick good-bye kisses, frustrating the hell out of both of us crush-laden writers.

W. D. was a dreamy beauty like no other, an ethereal power-house with cleavage existing to be licked and succored, with lips lightly painted with the brownish "Terra" by Mac, that begged for attention. Those lips, Stacey and I agreed, should have been on view alongside the *Mona Lisa* at the Louvre.

Stacey's fantasy was to kiss W. D. slowly in a field of wild grass with her fist inside of our beloved agent. Mine was to watch W. D. masturbate while I read poetry to her.

Unimaginative at best, right? Considering that she was married to a guy who was a Triple Scorpio.

Still, we were game. That evening, after checking into our sepa-rate rooms at the Four Seasons, we took a cab downtown to meet W. D. at Nobu. Imagine our surprise when seated next to her was a lanky looking dude in his late twenties, with long black hair and un-usually gray eyes, who wore a pair of black-framed glasses that gave him a decidedly artsy appearance.

"That *can't* be her husband. Whoever he is, he better not be a sculptor," Stacey muttered as we approached the table.

After two bottles of wine, dessert, and a last glass of port for each of us, Stacey continued her flirtathon with W. D., as Patrick, her assistant, and I took turns reciting the lyrics to every Led Zeppelin song ever written. Patrick, it turned out, played bass in a rock band in Berkeley. I wanted him to hear my brother's band, D'Haene. I just happened to have a copy of his new CD, *Brother Man*, in my room.

Throughout dinner Patrick's leg bounced against mine several times, and I was dying to drag Stacey into the restroom to see what she thought. Of course, she'd probably think he wanted *her*, not me.

We all shared a cab back to the hotel, and Patrick asked me if I'd like to have a nightcap at the bar. Stacey and W. D. both wanted to call it a night, W. D. intimating that she wasn't used to drinking so much. We said our good nights and planned to reconvene in the lobby at eleven the next morning before our meeting at Penguin.

STACEY

W. D. did not let go of me as we strode toward the elevator. After we stepped inside, her fingers remained curled around my upper arm.

"What floor?" I asked.

"Eight," she answered.

"Ahh," I said, "my favorite number."

She laughed. "You?"

"I'm above you," I replied. "Twelve. But I'll see you to your room so you don't run into any trouble on the way, given your public drunkenness."

We both tittered, filling the elevator with a certain kind of expansive, shared glee.

When we arrived at her room, she fished out her key card from her bag and I reached for it.

"Allow me," I invited.

I slid the key card into the slot and opened the door. Dim lights greeted us along with a bed prepared for sleep—or other nocturnal activities—along with a pair of enticing chocolates perched on the bed's two pillows.

W. D. dropped her purse, kicked off her high heels, and giggled. "Oh, how generous! They left me *two* chocolates instead of one."

This was no time to be shy. She was my *agent*, after all.

"Maybe they understand a woman as exceptional as you should never spend the night alone," I said.

Another giggle tripped from her throat as she turned her back away from me and surprisingly asked me to unzip her dress, while she released herself from her black pumps.

"Oh . . . my pleasure," I managed.

She slipped out of the tight dress, turned and stood before me wearing only a short black slip. My eyes drifted to her spectacular legs.

"Get out! You are smoking hot!" I exclaimed.

"Oh, come on now," she said, and then let out a throaty laugh. "What can I get you? I have a whole minibar!"

"Uh, sure. I can stay for a drink."

"What will it be?"

"Whatever you're having," I responded

"I'm so tipsy already it would be dangerous for me to have any more wine."

Dangerous? I didn't know what to think that meant, so I said: "Let's really go wild and have seltzer."

W. D. handed me a fresh drink and excused herself as she headed to the restroom. My mind racing, I eased myself onto the creamy leather couch. I could hear W. D. humming a tune in the bathroom. Strangely, I had used Richard's words: "smoking hot," at her completely unexpected unveiling. She *had* stroked my arm throughout dinner, leaning closer over and over, brushing her shoulder against mine several times. But what had it meant?

As I waited, a wild image came to my mind of her long, reckless tresses streaming over my body like waves. A tingling sensation trickled through my being. Then I was struck with the image of those Louvre lips approaching mine.

(What!? For real? Gup-head, I'm making a run for it!)

However, my body stayed put as the bathroom door opened and W. D. stepped out wearing even less than her black slip. My eyes were transfixed by the gleaming pearls around her neck. Otherwise, I was paralyzed by her completely naked self.

We stared at each other. I rose from the couch and stepped toward her as if in a work of fiction. Could this pre-Raphaelite vision be real?

"Remember," she whispered, "when you sent me your first novel, *Dive*?"

I nodded, unable to speak.

"I read it in one sitting," she continued, "overwhelmed, completely captured by your prose. I knew then that one day I'd be standing in front of you like this."

Words left my vocabulary as W. D. moved closer to me. Luckily, my body was not rendered wordless. My hands lifted and reached into the rivulets of her straw-colored locks. Her fingers glided around my waist and we came together like soft morning glory petals closing at dusk.

The wine no longer intoxicated me—I was now drunk from the beguiling wonder of a woman in my arms for the first time ever. My palm cupped her cheek, those lips so close to mine it seemed impossible to breathe.

"Dive, dive, dive," she murmured.

She quoted my book from memory: *"Let the wind in. . . . I wonder if she means that some moments are so still, it seems like they vanish before they really even exist. . . .'"*

I was stunned as my fingers trailed down her neck, across her shoulders, alighting on the smooth round pearls draped above her mesmerizing breasts. My head tilted forward without my even knowing and our lips brushed against each other's.

We parted briefly as she whispered more of my work: *"I wonder where she came from. I wonder if she's real. Because as this stranger walks by, my mouthful of unanswered questions vanishes. There's never been anything like this woozy, wonderful breath. . . .'"*

Our mouths and tongues met. (Gup Girl, have you ever imagined that the ocean existed inside of you? That the place where all life began is now *you*? No wonder I love the sea so goddamn much!)

To press against her with my body, my hands, and my mouth instantly redefined the world as I knew it.

This was a WOMAN.

As we kissed, W. D.'s hands floated up my torso, over my shoulders, along my arms until her hands met mine, once again lost in her hair. As if our fingers were deciding what our future would be, they moved to my slinky black top and lifted it up over my head.

I wore a sheer red brassiere, the fabric so diaphanous that it revealed my budding nipples.

"'What have I been so afraid of? Not this part. The part when the sound of her voice plunges into my heart; the mention of her name like a dagger in my chest is what frightens me. . . . As if I'm underwater, as if I have dived into a pool and rise, laggardly, unbreathing, to the surface . . .'" she murmured.

The sound of my words in her voice fired through me. They propelled us closer to those chocolates than either one of us might have ever imagined. Arms and legs rolling and twining, our bodies undulated against each other's as our tongues dove deeper. All at once, W. D. was on top of me. She lifted herself away from our kiss and deftly unclasped the front of my bra, teasing the material across my breasts until they were fully exposed.

Again, we stared at each other, and I realized that our slits were pressed together in the most phenomenal way. It was as if our hearts were beating against each other's. W. D. slowly lowered her torso, then her breasts, onto mine. A groan that I did not recognize rose in me, vaulted through me as her lips returned to mine. She captured the sound, then offered her own moan of pleasure for me to swallow.

We stayed there, pulsing, barely moving, mesmerized, until it became unbearable. My pants came off as if they were soaring in flight. I rolled on top of her, feeling again that foreign sensation, nothing as insistent as a cock between us. Instead, like the same petals of the luscious flower that had been our lips earlier—opening and closing, seeking and beseeching—the mystery of who we really were was momentously revealed.

I was her and she was me.

ELISE

At 3 A.M, Patrick and I ordered a pizza and grabbed six more beers from the minibar. Engaging in air guitar could really work up an appetite. A dream of mine had come true: For one long, reckless night I was a fifteen-year-old boy rockin' out with my best bud.

No matter how cute he was, I had decided while we were at the hotel bar to save my luscious libido for my reunion with C. Besides, Patrick—"Trick," my new name for him—and I were far more turned on to the cacophony of rock n' roll than each other.

I was only sorry that Stacey hadn't joined us and was alone in bed, and that she had missed out on my teenage wasteland. I vowed to try some other way to get her mind off of Jocko. Even though she had put her best flirtatious face forward tonight with W. D., underneath it all I sensed her lingering heartache. I almost felt guilty for not asking her if she wanted to talk.

Instead, I decided to get hot with Hendrix tonight, clamor with Clapton, jones on Journey, bellow to Boston, lurch to the Led, and strum to the Stones—I could go on and on, but you get the picture. As for my brother's band, Trick agreed: "The cure for the common rock!" There was something to finding a musical soul mate that even transcended the high of sex. Well . . . almost.

(Note to Writing Partner: Let's make one of our LAME DUCK characters a quack star.)